WHEELER'S
CHOICE

WHEELER'S CHOICE

CHOICE

JERRY BUCK

M. EVANS
Lanham • Boulder • New York • Toronto • Plymouth, UK

Published by M. Evans
An imprint of Rowman & Littlefield
4501 Forbes Boulevard, Suite 200, Lanham, Maryland 20706
www.rowman.com

10 Thornbury Road, Plymouth PL6 7PP, United Kingdom

Distributed by National Book Network

British Library Cataloguing in Publication Information Available

Library of Congress Cataloging-in-Publication Data

The hardback edition of this book was previously cataloged by the Library of
Congress as follows:

Buck, Jerry,
    Wheeler's Choice / Jerry Buck.
      p. cm.—(An Evans novel of the West)
    I. Title. II. Series.
    PS3552.U3328W47   1989   89-17228
    813'.54—dc20 ·

ISBN: 978-1-59077-336-9 (pbk. : alk. paper)
ISBN: 978-1-59077-337-6 (electronic)

∞™ The paper used in this publication meets the minimum requirements of
American National Standard for Information Sciences—Permanence of
Paper for Printed Library Materials, ANSI/NISO Z39.48-1992.

Printed in the United States of America

For Carol,
  who is my choice,

And to her father,
  Ben Boese,
  who lent his first name,

And to the memory of my father,
  Harold Campbell Buck,
  a cattle rancher as flinty
  as Angus Finlay.

Chapter One

Truly, we were in the bowels of the earth. Squeezing us, inching us forward in the blackness and the wet and the cold. I could feel the closeness, the pressure building. Ready to propel us through. We were ready. Oh, God, we prayed for release! We prayed for escape! We prayed for freedom!

Once again I awkwardly raised the wooden plank and shoved it into the damp earth. The clayey soil was stubbornly unyielding and my strength was nearly spent, but I felt the sharpened end of the makeshift shovel penetrate an inch or so. An inch closer to the end. An inch closer to *freedom!* An inch closer to completing the tunnel.

Freedom lay at the end of the tunnel, and we had to finish it. We had to drive this underground passage from our barracks, past the stockade fence, past the pickets, to the waiting green fields. There we could climb back into the fresh air and the light. Back into the world.

Whenever we weren't digging, we plotted our escape route.

The majority, led by Moses Thatcher, favored going north to Canada. Old Moses would look up at me from his book of Blackstone and say, "It's pure logic, Ben Wheeler. The Yanks expect us to turn south toward home, but we hightail it to Canady." The rest, egged on by Timothy Stevens, wanted to head south, cross the Ohio into Kentucky, push on to Virginia, and get back to fighting for Jeff Davis and Robert E. Lee.

It's not that we didn't want to take up arms again. It's that we figured we stood a better chance by going through Canada. Lord knows, I wanted to get back into it. I'd been in this hellhole the Yankees called Camp Chase for more than a year. I'd been riding with Major Mosby's Partisan Rangers back when we were on our own and later when we joined up with the 43rd Battalion and Jeb Stuart's boys. I took a shine to Jeb Stuart, just like I had to Mosby. I guess I stood a head taller'n either one, but they both had the itch for a fight.

When a bluebelly guard told me they killed Stuart at a place called Yellow Tavern, it got me some riled. His real mistake was to laugh about it. He ain't likely to laugh again for a long time. I spent six weeks in the Hell Box in the summer sun. Ohio gets mighty hot and mighty humid in the summer. It was worth it to wipe the smile off that bluebelly's face. Moses gave me holy hell when I got out. He said digging the tunnel was more important than revenge. My mind told me he was right, but my heart wouldn't agree.

Moses was like a pa to me, more so than my own pa, God rest his tormented soul. I had been reading law with Moses, using the few books he had managed to save. Every night, when I wasn't in the tunnel digging, we talked about it. Over and over he told me, "Don't just learn the law, Ben. Learn respect for the law, too. Law ain't much good to nobody if you stick to the letter of the law and ignore the spirit."

Moses was too old and too weak to dig in the tunnel, but he was our leader and inspiration. In the past few months the consumption had been on him something terrible. But he had a mind like a fiercely burning fire. Get near him and you could feel the warmth of his intellect. Moses said I had a feeling for the law. All I knew was that it had a way of taking the rage and wildness out of me. Of course, Abby's had a lot to do with taming me down, too.

Abby comes in with the Quaker ladies. Abigail Carter was her name. The bluebellies didn't much like it, but them Quaker ladies run over them like Mosby's Rangers riding through the Yankee pickets in Loudoun County.

My eyes were closed to keep the dirt out, but if I opened them I still

2

would have been blind. I could not see my hands in front of my face, or the makeshift shovel my hands were holding. The darkness in the tunnel was the blackest black I had ever seen. A frightening black that turned your gut to ice. An enveloping black that gripped your throat and tightened it and stifled the scream struggling to get out.

I twisted the plank and broke off a few chunks of soil. I felt it with my fingers, then shoved the dirt back between my body and the walls of the tunnel.

I was facedown in the tiny, cramped tunnel. I could only work the shovel by extending it awkwardly ahead of me. Yet I hardly felt the ache in my arms and body. It had long ago turned to numbness. I was nearly naked, to protect my uniform, and the damp cold went through my flesh to my bones. My lungs ached from breathing the foul, oxygen-starved air.

I pressed my body against one side of the tunnel so that I could speak to the man behind me.

"Bring up the light," I whispered.

We never talked above a whisper in the tunnel and tried to muffle the sounds of our digging. We knew the Yanks had listening posts to detect an escape tunnel. They had every right to be suspicious. We had tried before and been caught.

The man behind me passed the whispered command along. Then I heard nothing more.

I thrust the plank against the soil again and broke off a few more pieces of dirt. As I shoved the dirt back, a yellowish glow penetrated the blackness, and the flickering candle was passed up to me. Even the faint light from the candle hurt my eyes. I held out the candle and surveyed the work I had done in the last hour. I couldn't tell much, but I particularly wanted to inspect the roof of the tunnel to see if there was any sign of weakness. We'd have to shore it up quickly. The Yanks never figured out why the barracks were so cold. We cut up most of the firewood to make shoring for the tunnel.

"Bring up the measure," I said.

"On the way," the man behind me whispered.

He pushed the rope into my hands, and I pulled it tight against the raw end of the tunnel. The rope was a rigging of every piece of hemp and cloth we could get our hands on. It appeared to be more knots than anything. Every piece was joined by a granny knot, and every measurement was marked by a slip knot.

"How much?" came the anxious whisper behind me.

"How much?" he pleaded again. He tried inching himself forward in the tiny space between my body and the tunnel wall.

I estimated the distance from the last knot to where my thumb and finger pressed the rope to the dirt. I looked back at the man's tense face. It was nearly covered by beard, and what the beard didn't hide of his flesh the dirt did. His haunted eyes stared at me from the blackness.

"Five inches," I said. "Five inches or pret' near."

The face behind me broke into a gap-toothed grin. I hadn't recognized Bill Avery in the darkness until that moment. As Bill passed the word back, I tied a knot in the rope. Later, we'd slip the knot to gain a few inches of rope.

I went back to hacking at the dirt. I was weakening and not making much headway. In a while I felt Avery tug at my leg.

"Moses says it's time," he said in a hoarse whisper.

Those were welcome words. I began to back out of the tunnel.

The Yankees counted noses three times a day. We'd gone into the tunnel as soon after the noon count as we could. I had no idea what time it was. You lose track of time in the darkness because there is nothing to relate to. Even if you carried a pocket watch and a candle to read it by, time seemed unreal in the tunnel.

That night, huddled around the potbellied stove, we talked of home and the war and loved ones. It was cold in the barracks, and outside a harsh February wind, gathering speed since Lake Erie, picked up the snow on the ground and hurled it against the wooden sides of the barracks like grapeshot.

I was reading one of Moses's precious law books. He had started the war with enough books to fill a knapsack. Now he had only five, and three of those were held together by string. We guarded them as zealously as we did the tunnel. Moses had been a lawyer in Tennessee, and when the war came he enlisted as a private. I didn't know how old he was, but I knew he'd had a grandson who was a colonel with Lee.

One of the prisoners, with a glazed look in the eye, whispered conspiratorially, "I hear'd it today. Fella from Alabam, two huts down tol' me." He looked around suspiciously. "Says ol' Robert E. hisself is comin' to bust us out. Says he's done passed Harper's Ferry and's most to Wheelin'. Be here—"

Moses, mending a tear in his jacket, stopped him. "Hush, you old fool," he said. "You gonna get everybody all riled up for nothin'. Lee ain't goin' nowheres. He's got his hands full just holdin' off Useless S. Grant. So stop spreadin' that fool—"

Moses was seized by a racking cough.

He couldn't stop, and it nearly doubled him up. I put down the law book I had been reading and got the tin cup of water from the top of the stove. I poured a little down his throat. The hot water usually eased the coughing. It was the only remedy we had. Sometimes, when he was spitting up blood, it didn't do any good at all.

He wiped his mouth with the back of his hand and smoothed his white beard. "Thank you, Ben," he said. "Sometimes I think the consumption is going to get me down."

"Don't talk like that," I said. "Before you know it, we're going to finish that tunnel and you're going to be in Canada and get some real medical treatment."

Moses shook his head. "I don't know, Ben. I swear it looks hopeless sometimes."

"That's the ailment talking," I said. "There ain't nothing hopeless, Moses. You told me that yourself. Lord knows, you told me that enough times. And what better example you got right here than me, Ben Wheeler?

"I was headed straight for hell. Wild and mean and reckless. Ran away from home when I was a pup. Punched cows in Texas. Carried a tin star a time or two. Shames me to say it, but I also worked the other side of the law. I was a right smart gunfighter. Maybe not too smart. The only reading I did was on a whiskey label, and my community spirit was shooting up the saloon on Saturday night. You turned me round, Moses. You turned me round. Maybe not completely—I still got lotsa piss an' vinegar in me—but you done it."

Moses laughed with just the tiniest cough following it. "I'm politician enough to want to claim all the credit I can get away with, Ben. But the fact is I can't claim it all. Don't forget Abby. She done her share—and then some!"

In the past year, Moses and his books had become more precious to me than life. More important than the tunnel. More profound than the war. It was the first time I had found a purpose to my life.

But the dearest and sweetest thing of all was Abby. "You will be a man of the law when the war's over," Abby told me during her visits to the prison camp. She came in with the Quaker ladies, but she wasn't one of them. Presbyterian, I was to learn.

Other women I had known had aroused only lust in me. I could not think an impure thought in Abby's presence. I felt at peace in her presence. The rage left me. She was the gentlest woman I had ever known. She thought only of helping others. Yet, I don't think she had reached her eighteenth birthday.

She talked to me about farming. Her pa raised corn, just like my pa did when I was a young'un back in Virginia. Our place was in the mountains, more rock than soil, and Pa brewed most of the crop into corn liquor. He was his own best customer, and it didn't improve his disposition none. He had the rage, too. I expect that's where I got it.

She also talked to me of peace. Abby had more in mind than just the end of the war. "You just can't pick up a gun when somebody does you wrong," she said.

"I'm supposed to turn the other cheek?" I asked.

"Don't mock the Bible," she admonished. "You must learn to control your temper. You can accomplish more by control and reason than by letting your temper run wild."

I shrugged. "I been wild all my life."

"Yes, I know," Abby said, "and you must be proud of it to brag like that."

"I wasn't bragging," I said in protest, then fell into shamed silence. I had been bragging and I had been proud of it. That's what a man did.

"There's more to being a man than fighting and carrying a gun," she said. There were times when I would swear she could read my mind.

"Who is the braver—and the wiser?" she asked. "A man who takes offense at every imagined slight, or the man who overlooks petty offenses and is able to forgive? My pa says it takes more courage to hold back than to charge in with fists flying." She laughed. "He calls it 'intestinal fortitude.' But once when he didn't know I was around, I heard him call it 'guts.'"

I had found my tongue again. "A man's got to stand up for what he thinks is right."

"Of course," she said, "and I'll stand there beside you. All I'm saying, Ben Wheeler, is the time for wildness is past and you have to keep your temper in check."

6

I was so enthralled by Abby that I didn't see the guard until I felt the point of his bayonet under my chin. The bayonet was at the end of his Spencer, and he was holding it as if he'd like nothing better than to run me through.

"What the hell you doin' talkin' to a woman, Johnny Reb?" the guard demanded. He shoved the bayonet tighter against my skin.

Abby jumped to her feet. "He has every right to talk to me," she declared. "Now you put that knife and gun down this instant! Sergeant Wheeler is a gentleman."

The guard eyed her suspiciously. "Y'sticken' up for a Reb agin yer own kind?"

He turned his scorn against her. He said. "Wait'll th' lieutenant hears we got a southern sympathizer here. Playin' up to them Rebs like some kinda dance hall floozy."

My hand was on the bayonet shaft, and I had it aside, ready to wrestle the rifle from the guard's hands.

But Abby had anticipated my move. "Stop it!" she shouted. "Stop it, both of you!"

The commotion had attracted the attention of the prisoners nearby and of several of the Quaker ladies.

The three of us—Abby, the guard, and myself—were in a circle of anxious faces. Abby spoke first.

"I'm afraid the sentry tripped," she explained. "Sergeant Wheeler reached out to prevent his fall."

A Yankee lieutenant pushed his way through the crowd. He looked at Abby, then me, and finally the guard. "The lady said you tripped, Private Biggens. Is that what you say?"

Private Biggens studied the ground for a moment. "Yes, sir," he said finally. "That's what happened. I tripped."

"Let's break it up," the lieutenant said. "You prisoners know you ain't permitted to bunch up on the grounds. Move along. Private Biggens, get back to your post. And, ladies, I do believe you have duties tending to the sick."

He moved closer to me and said in a half whisper, "You ain't fooling nobody, Wheeler. You come this close"—he held a finger a hairsbreadth from his thumb—"to getting the Hell Box! You better keep your nose clean!"

After the lieutenant walked off, Abby smiled and said, "See, you don't have to wrestle in the mud. Or end up in the—" She hesitated before saying the word "Hell Box."

A coquettish smile crossed her face. "I would not like you in the"— again a pause—"Hell Box. I'll be back next Saturday."

Chapter Two

In mid-March there was a sudden break in the weather. The icy winds stopped whistling down from Canada across Lake Erie, and the snow stopped. It seemed a miracle, and when, shortly before noon, the sun came out from behind the gray clouds, I knew it was a genuine godsend.

"Fetch me my hat," Moses said. "I'm goin' outside."

He threw back the thin cover on his cot and tried to rise. By sheer determination he got up on his elbows.

"Let me move the bed by the window," I suggested. Moses had grown weaker every day as his cough grew stronger.

"It may be th' last time I'll see the sun," he said, still pushing with all his might to rise from the bed.

"You stubborn old coot," I said, admitting defeat, and helped him to sit up. I put his shoes on for him. Like the rest of us, he slept fully clothed because of the terrible cold.

I sat him on a box beside the barracks, and he raised his face to the sun. About five or six others came and sat with us. For the longest time we sat there without speaking. I didn't want to engage him in conversation for fear it would start him coughing.

He turned his pale face from side to side, absorbing the sun's rays. After a while, he said, "Maybe it's an omen."

I was soaking up the warmth, too, and half dreaming. "What?" I said.

"I said, maybe it's an omen. The sunshine. I think it means we're going to break into the sunshine."

"We are in the sunshine," I said, my mind still wandering a bit.

"The real sunshine, my boy. The *real* sunshine. The sunshine we'll see when we come up through the tunnel. God's provenance. *Freedom!*"

"You got that right, Moses," said Liam Murphy.

Liam had fled a famine in Ireland and had not been off the boat in Charleston a month when the South fired on Fort Sumter. He had strolled down to the waterfront that April morning to watch the shelling that had begun before dawn. Before the end of the day, he was loading shells onto boats supplying Fort Moultrie. By the end of the week he was in uniform.

"The end of the week," he said. "I 'spect by th' end of the week we'll sashay through that tunnel—and find a grand rainbow at th' end." He chuckled. Liam was the damnedest optimist I'd ever run into. I knew he was dead wrong, but we needed our spirits lifted.

"Irishman, I think you could sell snake oil to th' devil hisself," said Simon Keller. "'Member that tunnel we started in 'sixty-three? Wal, y'wasn't here then, but it rained like hell and it collapsed. Next one we no more'n got th' shaft dug and th' Yanks found it. Same for the one after that."

"Aye," said Liam, "but we're past th' fence this time. Th' measure tells us that."

Simon snorted. "Sumpun'll happen, you wait and see. Allus does. It'll rain. It'll collapse. Or the bluebellies'll find it."

Poke Bradley took a blade of dry grass from his mouth and said, "It don't matter nohow."

We all turned and looked at Poke. Nobody knew what his real name was.

Poke, seeing he had our attention, continued, "You know them Quaker ladies what come in here. You know 'em, Ben. That gal you sweet on comes in with 'em."

"Abigail Carter, a right fair lass," Liam interrupted. All eyes turned on me, and I blushed.

"Anyhow, one of them Quaker ladies told me Grant's knockin' at Jeff

Davis's door. Says he'll be in Richmond 'fore the next moon.''

"Sheeeet!" cried Bill Avery. "You start believin' them lies the Yanks feed us, you liable to believe anythin'. Next moon! I think you *tetched* by the moon!"

"Never knowed a Quaker to lie," said Poke.

Moses, coughing slightly, said, "You gotta have faith. My pa was at Valley Forge. He had faith. So did the boys with him. Robert E. Lee, he got faith. And I got faith. You mark my word, we gonna finish that tunnel, and we gonna march out of here with our heads held high. And we gonna—"

He was unable to finish as the coughing grew worse. He doubled over, his whole body shaking from the effort. He pressed a hand to his mouth, and it was quickly covered with blood.

As I picked him up, I said, "I got the faith, Moses. I'm gonna take you through that tunnel, and I'm not going to stop until I reach Canada and find a proper doctor for you."

Abby held a damp cloth to his head, trying to cool the fever. Moses had not been out of his bed in more than a week. The weather had turned foul again, but I spent most of my time beneath the earth. Digging, digging, digging. We were close, agonizingly close, but we couldn't go up until we were safely past the pickets.

She placed a hand to his forehead. "He's burning up," she said quietly. Moses had been in and out of consciousness, and she didn't want him to hear. "I can't bring the fever down. I fear for his life."

I said, "He's got to hang on. We don't have much further to go."

"Further to go?" Abby asked.

I couldn't tell her about the tunnel. She was a northern woman, although I trusted her explicitly. Still, knowledge of the tunnel was a burden I did not want to place on her.

Moses stirred and murmured. He opened his rheumy eyes. His breathing was labored, but at least he wasn't coughing. His lips were dry and he ran his tongue over them, but it was dry, too. Abby raised his head with one hand and with the other tilted a tin cup of water to his parched lips.

Moses reached out, clawing at the air until he found my hand. "Ben," he said with an effort, "I want you to have 'em."

I wasn't sure at first what he was talking about.

"My law books," he said. "I want you to have 'em."

He tried to laugh, but it only caused him to strangle. Abby gave him another sip of water.

"Just like a lawyer, ain't it?" he said. "Dyin' without a will. I make my will to you and to Abby. With God as my witness."

He tried to tighten the grip on my hand. His hand was terribly hot and had little strength in it. "I want you to take them and build a life with them," he said feebly. "You got a feel for the law, boy. You study them books and you'll be somebody."

He lapsed into unconsciousness again.

"He's right," said Abby. "You can be somebody."

"The war's changed everything," I said. "The South is losing. The North may never let us out of here."

"It will be a time of healing," she said. "You can be one of the healers."

"I don't know," I said. "I been a hell-raiser all my life. A drifter. It's hard to change."

"You just need someone to help you along the way, the way Moses did," she said.

"I don't know anybody like that," I said. "Moses been like a pa to me. More like a pa than my real pa. He wasn't much of a father. He had an acquaintance with the bottle. The day my ma died he was dead drunk. Now Moses is about to leave this world. I don't know of anybody to help me."

The only sound was Moses's labored breathing.

After a long silence, I heard Abby say, "I do."

I couldn't answer. Suddenly my throat went dry. Did she say what I thought she said? I didn't want to ask her. I was afraid of breaking the spell.

Moses died before the sun came up. He simply stopped breathing. I felt a tear in my eye. I couldn't recall ever having cried. I wiped the tear away, and I saw that Abby's face was also wet. Wordlessly we fell into each other's arms. The emotions bombarded me, one after another. I was sad, I was angry, I was bitter, I was afraid, I was confused.

We buried Moses the next day. The Quaker ladies sang hymns, and Zachary Smith, who had done a little preaching, said the words over his grave.

The day after that, Petersburg and Richmond fell. We didn't hear about it for three days. There was no denying it this time. The guards were tickled pink and unable to resist taunting us.

"Abe Lincoln's sitting in Jeff Davis's office," sang one guard. "Where's Jeff Davis?"

"Hidin' out with Robert Elite," said another.

In the next five days, before Lee surrendered at Appomattox, we kept digging. Every inch brought us closer to our goal.

Bill Avery spoke for all of us. "I don't give a shit. I'd rather go out through the tunnel with my head held high than go home through the front gate with my tail between my legs."

In the end we didn't have much choice. Try as we could we could not complete the tunnel. At least not before the prison camp commandant spoke to us at roll call and said we had been paroled.

Outside circumstances had at last brought us the freedom we had so desperately sought. Lee's surrender meant our freedom. It seemed like history was playing a cruel joke on us.

As I wrapped up my few belongings and tied up Moses's precious law books in a makeshift knapsack, I wondered about the future. I wondered if there was a future. I looked at Moses's well-thumbed copy of Blackstone, and my mind conjured an image of him sitting by the window, looking for all the world like Papa Christmas with his snow-white hair and beard. "You have no future," I said bitterly. "You don't even have a present. They robbed you of that."

I tried to choke back the bitterness and see it as Moses would have seen it. Moses had always told me to forgive, but I wasn't certain that I could.

Outside the camp I faced north toward Canada. Should I go in that direction? I faced south. I was not sure I wanted to go in that direction, either. I did not want to think of what the South would be like in defeat and living under the conqueror's boot.

I pulled out the piece of paper Abby had given me. It was a note in her fine handwriting. It told me how to reach her home. Abby lived to the west of the camp. She also wrote that she loved me. Nobody had ever told me that before.

I knew the direction I was going.

Chapter Three

It was the last week of July when Angus Finlay rode into Colchester, Kansas, with three thousand head of cattle and a dozen thirsty cowhands.

The little town, just over the border from the Nations, had been home to Abby and me for nearly four years. I was marshal and had worn a badge in a few other places since I'd claimed Abby as my bride at the end of the war.

Angus had just come up the Chisholm Trail through the Indian Territory, and before his visit to the bathhouse he was covered with all the accumulated dirt of the drive. He was a bowlegged little man, with sandy hair, a huge mustache, a permanent squint, and blue eyes, the kind that bore right through you and just naturally made you want to tell the truth. They're the kind of eyes I could have used as marshal. I don't think Angus stood more than an inch higher than Major Mosby, even in his high-heel boots, and Lord knows he could be just as cussed. Angus was as sturdy and rock-hard as the Scottish Highlands that birthed him, and no amount of living on the range would ever still the burr that rolled over his tongue like the River Clyde.

Angus could squeeze a double eagle until it screamed or roll a cartwheel farther than any man I knew, as his Gaelic ancestry might imply, but he was a fair man and generous with his friendship. He kept an eye on his hands, settled their mischief, and he and I hit it off.

We'd become fast friends two years before, when Angus's herd arrived before another trail crew had left. I spent much of that night breaking up bar fights between the rival cowhands and hoping nothing more serious would erupt. My appeal to the first trail boss was ignored. But Angus waded in, chided his own men, and put the fear of God into the other crew.

Colchester was just a few miles inside Kansas and was the first place a thirsty cowhand could get a drink after crossing the Indian Territory. The church folks swore Osage Street was solid saloons from one end to the other. I would have vouched for that myself whenever a drive reached town and bedded down for a few days before going on to Abilene or Dodge City. The cowhands, after a month or so of enforced sobriety, loaded up on cheap whiskey, and those who didn't immediately get sick or pass out usually got into a brawl or shot up Osage Street. My job was to see that they didn't hurt themselves, and especially to see that they didn't hurt any townspeople.

The hands just wanted to let off steam, and, having ridden for a few brands myself, I knew the feeling. Some trail bosses were as rambunctious as a cowhand who had been eating dust on drag all the way from the Brazos River. Angus was an exception, and when he got to town I rarely had to worry about his crew.

Angus was an elder in the Presbyterian Church, and like many another God-fearing drover, he would not permit profanity by his men. A simple "hell" or "damn" brought a fine of five cents. Stronger language was dealt with accordingly. And woe betide the man caught playing a game of chance while eating off his chuck. Angus looked upon gambling as the devil's own doings. Nevertheless, Angus was not only respected and feared by his hands, but beloved as well. They would follow him through the gates of hell.

"West Texas," he said one night as he dug into Abby's beef and potatoes. "Aye, Ben, there's the place for a man. 'An honest man aboon his might.' A bit of Bobby Burns, but it's nae Caledonia. Texas has room for a man to make himself to home. And no laird to answer to. We could use a man like you to bring law and order to San Miguel. A drunken cowboy shot the marshal two winters ago and we've never found a replacement. Have to rely on the sheriff in Logantown."

"Law and order?" said Abby, arching her eyebrows. "Why, Mr. Finlay, I don't believe you've heard a thing we've been saying. Ben has been reading the law since Moses Thatcher made him acquainted with it, and the time has come for him to open his practice."

"You mean practice the law without backing it up with a six-gun?" Angus asked. He turned to me as he said it, winking with the eye away from Abby.

Abby detected the wink but chose to ignore it. She said, "There will always be rogues who live by the gun, Mr. Finlay. Ben has done his duty as a lawman, but the times are changing. It's time for him to give up his badge and become a man *of* the law."

I laughed and said, "What Abby means, Angus, is that it's time I started enforcing the law in a courtroom instead of on a dusty cow town street. Mostly, I just take care of rowdy cowhands looking for a little fun after the long drive from Texas. Although I must say you keep yours pretty much in tow. Still, it can get a little more serious now and then."

Abby eyed me as she poured the coffee. She kept her thoughts to herself, but I knew what they were. Guns had been a natural part of my life since I lit a shuck from Virginia to Texas when I was still a pup. I had a Colt .36-caliber ball-and-percussion revolver, which I had relieved from a gentlemen one night on the journey, and a trusty companion she was in those wild times before I rode back East to join Mosby and his Rangers. I had been marshal in Colchester for nearly four years, and before that there had been other cow towns. And in that time there had been a few tight moments. Once, when I was chasing a bandit through a winter storm, Abby stayed up for three nights, convinced she was going to become a widow. I didn't want to do that to her again.

"So," I said, "I've given the town council notice that I'm turning in my badge. I'm going to practice law."

"Aye, we have need of them, too," said Angus, ignoring the napkin in his lap and wiping his long sandy mustache with the tip of the red checkered bandanna around his neck. "Texas is a bonny place. A man with a legal turn of mind could make a name for himself."

I took another bite of the meat and potatoes and studied my fork for a moment before swallowing. I said, "I'll give the council formal notice when the last herd comes through at the end of summer. We're looking for a place to set down roots, Angus. Tell me about this place of yours. San Miguel, is it?"

I knew a thing or two about Texas, but the spreads I rode for were along the Gulf Coast. The farthest west I had been was San Antone.

We talked by the fire for hours until it was reduced to embers and Abby had long since gone to bed. Angus produced a bottle of whisky from his possibles bag. It was the smoothest I had ever tasted, and unlike the bourbon I was used to, it had a smoky taste that lingered on the tongue. Scotch whisky, he called it, and raising his glass to me, he said, *"'John Barleycorn got up again, and sore surprised them all.'"*

Finally Angus had to return to his herd, but by that time I had determined I would give San Miguel a try.

He told me of an unclaimed section on a little *rio* where I could raise a few head of cattle and Abby could plant a garden. I knew my first years as a lawyer would be lean ones, and I would need something to see us through.

Chapter Four

The remaining months of summer were hot and dry. For days on end the long cattle drives heading north to the railheads kicked up clouds of dust that cast a permanent twilight over the prairie and turned the sun a dull orange. The wind spread the dust across the land. It reddened the eye, choked the nose, dried the throat, and left a whitish film on clothing. It seeped into every house and building in Colchester. There was no escaping it. You ate it, sat in it, slept in it, breathed it. The grangers starting to crowd in from the east prayed for rain, but none came until September.

The herds coming into Colchester had grown fewer, and finally one day they stopped coming. I turned in my badge, sold our place to a pilgrim from Pennsylvania, loaded our meager belongings onto a wagon, and headed south to beat the first snow.

Several drovers told me of meeting Kiowa and Comanche bands in the Nations. One trail boss said he had lost several cows to about a dozen young Kiowa bucks spoiling for a fight.

So I kept my Winchester by my knee and a Sharps buffalo rifle at my feet. The Sharps was slow, but it was mighty permanent. It only took one slug from a Sharps to blow an Indian right off his mount.

Weeks before we had left I put Abby out behind the cabin and let her pop away with the Winchester until she became both fast and accurate. Abby had been born in Kentucky and grew up in Ohio and was no stranger to a rifle, despite her aversion to firearms.

We got off easy. The only hostiles we met were some enterprising Cherokees who demanded fifteen cents toll for crossing their land.

It took us just over three weeks to cross the rolling prairie land of the Indian Territory. We rarely made more than ten miles a day, and the numerous rivers and creeks that crisscrossed the territory slowed us considerably. Fording them was hard on Abby and the wagon. Thankfully, none was at flood stage at that time of year. Once we got past the two Canadians and the Washita, the going was easier.

There was no possibility of losing your way. The hooves of a million cows had dug a sunken road along the Chisholm Trail that even a blind man could follow. Or that blind man could follow his nose. There were enough cow flops to fertilize every farm in the state of Ohio.

Twenty-four days out of Colchester, we ferried across the Red River and entered Texas. Abby hadn't wanted to travel on the Sabbath, but I reminded her that we were in a race against the winter. We were on the go every day of the week.

Five days into Texas we felt the bite of the first norther at our backs. It blew day and night for the next week, chilling our bones and taxing our sanity with its relentless and ghostly moan over the sea of grass.

One morning, in the distance, by some grazing steers, I spied a windmill. It was spinning so furiously I remarked to Abby that it had dragged the well five miles across the prairie.

Abby smiled for the first time in weeks. "If only you could rig the quilts like sails," she said. "We could load the bullocks in back and sail all the way to San Miguel."

"Like a prairie schooner," I added.

We laughed at the welcome break in the tension caused by the wind. We camped early that day by a small stream, splashed happily in the frigid water, and made love for the first time since leaving Colchester.

As we drove west, the tall, nourishing buffalo grass of the north gradually gave way to the gama grass growing less densely in the sandy soil. The bullocks took to it like it was hay, and the roan and the buckskin I trailed behind the wagon kept their stomachs full. Texas herds grew fat on it.

Gradually, too, we began to enter tableland. In the distance we saw purple mesas, and behind them low mountains darkened by a thick growth of piñons.

We passed longhorns grazing on the grasslands. Several times we met ranch hands riding line. They were suspicious of strangers crossing their range and feared we might be tempted to butcher a cow to supplement our fare. I knew better than to poach on another man's land, but on numerous occasions we dined on rabbit and prairie chicken, and once on deer.

Abby's cheerful friendliness quickly allayed their suspicions, and there wasn't a cowboy among them who wasn't eager to accept her invitation to a home-cooked supper.

When at last I spotted Angus's Lazy A brand, I knew we had reached San Miguel.

I was wrong. Angus grazed his herds over such a vast area that it took another week to reach town.

It was then I realized I had underestimated Angus. He had spoken lightly of his "little spread," and judging from his unprepossessing appearance, I had taken him at his word. I had always figured part of the herd he drove north belonged to his neighbors. I saw now that Angus was only being modest. He was truly what the Texans called a cattle baron.

Chapter Five

Angus became not only my first client in San Miguel, but my patron as well. Ranchers and their families rode in from fifty miles to attend the barbecue he threw to introduce us to the community. It was one of those mild days on the high plains before the northers sweep snow down from Canada.

More than two hundred ranchers and townspeople gathered at the Lazy A Ranch, and Angus declared a holiday for his ranch hands.

Everyone was in a festive mood as they gathered behind the main house in an area Angus called a patio. It was paved with flat stones, decorated with flowering shrubs, some growing in big, gaily painted Mexican clay pots, and shaded by trees and an open lattice roof overgrown with wisteria.

Angus lived in a sprawling Spanish house made of adobe the color of earth. The summer heat never penetrated its three-foot-thick walls of dried adobe brick, and in the winter it was warm as toast. The roof had only the merest slant from the ridge to the eaves. Rather than the usual tile, it was three feet of dirt grown thick with grass, and was supported underneath by heavy timbers.

Angus, widowed and childless, was the grandee of this Spanish castle, but Juanita ran the household with a will of iron that even Angus adhered to. She was a short, dark Mexican woman who had the stamina of a longhorn steer and brooked about as much nonsense.

The women were to one side with Abby, to appraise her and see what new fashions she had brought down from Kansas. She wore a light blue chintz dress she had gotten by mail order from St. Louis. To ward off the cool air, she had draped over her shoulders a dark blue shawl she had knitted during those long nights she had waited for me to make my rounds and put the cowhands to bed. On her light brown hair she wore her best Sunday-go-to-meeting bonnet.

The ladies hadn't expected anything fancy, and they weren't disappointed. Abby, they saw as they sipped spiced tea, was plain folk just like them, and her lack of airs, her modesty, her cheeriness, plus her good sense, quickly won them over. Angus, who doted on her like a proud papa, frequently said, "That woman's got a head on her shoulders."

Now, when I said plain folk, I wasn't talking about Abby's looks. There was nothing plain there. She was a beauty, that's for sure. Angus called her his "bonny lass."

The men drifted over toward the cook house, where Ginger applied liberal dabs of a fiery sauce to a whole beef roasting over a fire of mesquite wood. A young Mexican turned the spit with a huge crank.

Lounging nearby on the cool grass was Ginger's dog, Caesar, a large, shaggy mongrel hound of unknown ancestry and an indeterminate shade of dirty yellow. Caesar had a disposition as surly as his master, and every man gave them both a wide berth. Ginger had a temper as volatile as his sauce, and with a brown derby perched on his head and red suspenders holding up his baggy pants, he stood by the spit like king of the hill.

Ginger had hair that matched his nickname, and his face seemed to be permanently flushed from too many choleric outbursts. Hard, sidelong glances warned the guests not to encroach upon his fiefdom. No man, not even Angus, presumed to impose upon Ginger until he was ready to dispense his culinary delights. On a roundup or on a trail drive a good cook was as essential to the morale of the cowhands as a pair of comfortable boots and an amenable cutting horse. And much more difficult to come by, so Angus gave Ginger his rein.

Near the house a group of cowboys sawed on fiddles and plucked at guitars and a banjo. They were loud and lively, if not always in tune.

At first I did not recognize "The Lakes of Killarney." Later I picked up strains of "Little Joe the Wrangler," "The Girl I Left Behind," and the inevitable "Old Chisholm Trail."

The men sized me up, as the women took their measure of Abby. It didn't take them more than an instant to see that I was no pilgrim. I'm a tall man, standing more than six feet, and my long legs were in a pair of wool pants and my feet were shod with my best pair of boots. Every ounce of fat had been sweated and pounded off my body, and I had that tiny, hard butt that a man develops when he spends his life in the saddle. I've got broad shoulders, long muscular arms, and eyes the color of an emerald.

Abby swore it was those cold green eyes and the way I looked at a man that kept me out of many a gunfight. I wasn't sure, being convinced that it was easier to stare a man down with piercing blue eyes. Most of the gunfighters I knew—that is, the ones who were good enough to still be alive—had blue eyes. Still, I always looked a man square in the eye when he was about to draw on me. You can back a man down that way, just the way a dog does. But if a man's bound and determined for a showdown, his eyes will also tell you when he's going to go for his gun.

A barrel-chested rancher, smelling of leather and horse sweat and clutching a tumbler of whiskey in one hand, broke the ice. He said, "Angus was right. You ain't no jackleg lawyer from one of them fancy eastern schools."

Everyone laughed at his left-handed compliment and took swigs of whiskey to moisten throats parched by the long ride to the party.

I agreed that I had gotten my education on the back of a mustang running through chaparral and curled mesquite for the Monarch brand down near Corpus Christi. "That's where I learned cow," I said. "After that, the law was easy."

They laughed again, and another stockman said, "Angus tells us you're a handy man with a Colt. We might have need of your services. We haven't had a marshal in San Miguel since a drunken drifter gunned down the last one two years ago. And the sheriff never seems to find his way to this neck of the woods. We could use a man who knows the business end of a Peacemaker. Not everyone in these parts knows how to respect another man's brand."

A short, wiry man with sparse hair and skin like old leather pushed his way through the ranchers and said, "What he means, Mr. Wheeler, is that some of the big ranchers got a handy way with a runnin' iron when it comes to the little fella's stock."

Out of the corner of my eye I saw the challenged man rest his right hand on his gun. Almost by instinct, I started to quell the trouble before it started, but I checked myself.

I was wearing neither a badge nor a gun now, and this was not my fight. For a stranger to step into a long-simmering feud would set both sides against me. Not even Angus would be able to keep my law practice from being aborted at birth.

I hadn't been in San Miguel two days before I learned that the most explosive issue on the range was the big ranchers vs. the little ranchers. Neither was too careful about whose steer they burned a brand on, and in recent years there had been much gunplay and more than a few men had stretched a rope hastily thrown over a tree branch.

I was surprised, however, to see a small rancher baiting a big rancher at a barbecue thrown by Angus Finlay, the biggest rancher of them all.

The banty rooster wasn't backing down. He, too, had his hand on his gun, and everyone else stepped back to clear a lane for the gunfire.

I hadn't known where Angus was when the trouble began, but he suddenly stepped beside the weather-beaten rancher and clasped a muscular arm around his shoulders.

"The trouble with you, Daniel, is that you think because your name's Daniel you gotta spend your whole life in the lion's den." Angus's voice was calm and friendly, and I'd swear the way the words r-r-r-rolled off his tongue like heather swaying in a breeze off the North Sea had something to do with taking the sting out of it.

"Why don't you step over here with me, Daniel, and I'll show you some whisky that was distilled on the banks of the Spey about the time that strapping son of yours was a wee bairn."

He walked the man over to a big oaken barrel and drew a glass for him. Angus soothed the man's anger as diplomatically and effortlessly as he handled his own rowdy cowhands. It was easy to see why Angus, despite his sometimes flinty nature, was the most respected and best-liked man in the territory.

Later, after I had put away my own share of Angus's smooth, smoky Scots whisky, he said to me in an aside, "You'll do all right, laddie. The ranchers, big and small, like you. And it was a smart thing you did to stay out of another man's fight. Aye, I saw your hands twitch and your jaw muscles screw up tight. You showed good judgment."

All the while his powerful hand was on my shoulder, though the top of his head reached no higher than my chin, and just as he had managed the wiry little cattleman, he steered me toward a man whose pink face and fancy duds told me he was no rancher. "Ben, I want you to meet somebody," he said. "This here's Otis Rankin, president of the Stockman's Bank."

I shook hands with Rankin, and I could tell by his iron grip and the straightforward way he looked me in the eye that he was a tougher man than he appeared. This was tough country, and only the toughest survived. Rankin, I could see, was thriving.

Before we sat down to enjoy slabs of spicy beef, red beans, and the hottest chili I had ever sampled, topped off by Ginger's wild berry cobbler, it was agreed that I would become the bank's counsel. Rankin offered me the use of an office on the second floor of the bank, which he proudly proclaimed to be the only brick building in San Miguel.

"Not adobe brick, mind you, but *gen-u-wine* red clay brick," he said. Rankin had a fat cigar clinched in the middle of his mouth, and he never moved it, not even to speak.

Angus winked at me. "He wants you close so he can keep an eye on you. And he'll charge you a stiff rent for that office, mark my word. Sometimes I think the man's a Scot."

Rankin curled his lips into a passable grin. The cigar sat in the middle of his face like an exclamation point.

Angus sniffed the air. It was thick with the mouth-watering aroma of the roasting beef. "I'd say the grub's about ready." He looked toward Ginger, who nodded his derby-topped head in agreement.

Angus picked up an iron rod and rang the triangle. It stopped nearly everyone in midconversation and brought them into a circle about the smoky, flavorful spit. Angus removed his hat and bowed his head. Beyond the circle came the squeals of children still at play. Angus didn't say a word, but after a moment several mothers shushed the kids and brought them to stand by their skirts.

Then Angus, who had never raised his head, began a long prayer that was almost fulsome in its supplications for the young couple come to their midst. More than once I remarked to Abby afterward that Angus's prayer was enough to see us through seven lean years.

Chapter Six

As Otis Rankin occasionally reminded me, I was not doing a land-office business in San Miguel. He also seldom failed to point out that I'd never become rich as a lawyer. But I handled enough liens, mortgages, contracts, bills of sale, and wills to pay our debts that first winter.

Otis, being a banker, put a great store by money. To me money was simply a tool. You used it if you had it, and if you didn't you found other means to get by.

I frequently stopped by Otis's desk in the bank to look over a deed or a contract. Often, he came up to my second-floor office by the steps inside the bank. His visits were never a surprise. You could hear him trudging up the steps, and when he got to the door he threw it open with a bang and came wheezing into my office.

The only excitement my first winter in San Miguel came when I defended two brothers accused of cattle rustling. They had been lucky enough to be tossed into the county jail to await the circuit judge without being the guests of honor at a necktie social. Nevertheless it was a foregone conclusion they would meet swift justice. It was my first case, and I lost.

No one held it against me that I had defended them. After the judge had sentenced the two boys to hang, an important rancher stopped me

outside the Bluebonnet Saloon, which had been our temporary court-room. He said, "It's a lawyer's duty to speak up for scoundrels."

I didn't say so publicly, but I knew the brothers' real crime was not rustling but being small ranchers who could not bend the law to their own devices the way the big ranchers did.

I expressed my feelings one night to Angus.

"Aye, lad, that's a fact," he replied. "How do you think the big ranchers here got so big? Nobody gave it to 'em, said, 'Here, this is yours.' By God, they *took* it! Every inch of land, every cow, every horse—everything that wasn't nailed down. And if it was nailed down, sometime they took that, too.

"When I came here in 'fifty-three, San Miguel was just a one-shack Indian trading post. Hardly had a name then. They just called it 'Doyle's Place,' after the sutler. I drove out five hundred head of cattle. Half of 'em I picked up on the way here. I didn't stop to ask whose cows they might be. I had three cowhands. I stopped here because there wasn't another soul in sight. I laid claim to everything I could see—and then some. And ever since then I've had to fight to keep it!"

Angus poured us each a couple fingers of his smoky whisky.

"Now, these two boys you defended," he said. "They're not a bad sort. I knew their daddy. They were just unlucky. They came along too late—and they got caught."

Abby and I wintered that first year in an adobe shack on the small spread I had staked claim to. Nothing was said, but I suspected that nobody challenged my claim because Angus wanted it that way.

Abby kept busy with her sewing and mending. She taught Sunday school at the tiny Presbyterian church where Angus was an elder. She fussed over the old widower as if she were his daughter, and he treated us both like the children he never had.

As soon as the ground had thawed enough to take a hoe, I turned over the soil and Abby planted a garden. She bought her seed at Asa Stanley's store, and I helped carry water from the creek. To my surprise, she had planted several rows of flowers. I never objected to this extravagance. Abby needed some beauty in her life. There was little enough in this hard land.

At night after supper, her sewing basket in her lap, she talked hopefully of starting a family. We had been on the move since that day I walked out of the Yankee prison and asked her to marry me. We stayed for a while in Ohio, then moved on to Indiana, where I learned I wasn't cut out for farming. I was a deputy for a few years in towns across Missouri. Then I was appointed marshal in Colchester.

After the northers slacked and died, I joined Angus on the spring roundup. His claim extended from the river to the eroded foothills and mesas seen distantly on the horizon. It was mostly flatlands, although in places it undulated like a washboard. Either way, it was laced with enough canyons and arroyos to keep his crew busy for weeks flushing out cows and their newborn calves.

My agreement with Angus was that I could keep one out of every four calves I brought in. By the time we finished burning the last brand on the last stray, I had a start. Certainly not a herd, or anything resembling a herd, but a good start. I devised my own brand, a kind of a running *W,* and I had Bob Dudley, the blacksmith, make the iron for me.

I was reluctant to see the roundup end. In a few weeks Angus would begin the drive north to Kansas, and I wouldn't see him again until he returned at the end of the summer.

A few days before he left, Abby baked sourdough bread and we went to visit. She also took along a jar of his favorite sour pickles. I know Abby would have made herself at home in the kitchen, too, were it not for Juanita's Spanish oaths. After supper, we played checkers and put away nearly a whole bottle of his Scots whisky. I hated to see Angus go, and secretly I envied him that dusty, sleepless, backbreaking, wondrously exiting ride north.

By steady work that summer, I built the house into a respectable home of three rooms. A few hundred yards behind it I built a corral, lashing together cedar poles with wet rawhide. When it dried to steellike hardness, no mustang or bull could tear it down.

In the fall, when a fire felt good again, Abby said to me of an evening, "It's a good life, Ben Wheeler."

I had a volume of Blackstone's *Commentaries* in my lap. I looked up at her as she darned a black sock. She was sitting in the Boston rocker we had carried from Kansas. The one I bought her because she said she wanted to rock our first child in it.

In the yellowish cast of the lamp, her skin was golden and flawless. Her light brown hair was silky, and her blue eyes were clear. She worked hard and she was tired. It grieved me that this harsh life, this harsh climate, and this heartless, unforgiving land would soon leave her skin as parched as the baked earth and would dull her hair. I had seen it in the other ranchers' wives.

I looked at her for a long time. Then I said, "Yes, Abigail Elizabeth Carter, it *is* a good life!"

She smiled and said, "Please, sir, do remember that I am an honest woman. Abigail Elizabeth Carter *Wheeler*!"

"An honest woman?" I said as I dropped the volume of Blackstone on the floor. "We'll see how honest you really are."

I gathered her in my arms, and the last thing she said as we stretched out on the blanket before the fire was, "*Quite* honest, to be honest."

Chapter Seven

Spring came suddenly our second year in San Miguel. One day the icy wind was cutting through to the bone. The next the bluebonnets were blooming on the plains. I spent the next six weeks in the saddle rounding up strays for Angus and chewing on Ginger's sonofabitch stew and red bean pie.

Before sunup every morning we gulped scalding coffee and wolfed bacon and fresh-baked sourdough biscuits. Angus drew an imaginary line down the center of every section, and at first light the cowboys fanned out in search of the steers. Ginger drove his chuck wagon along that center line, and in the afternoon we herded the cattle we had found toward the point where we figured Ginger had stopped.

As he rode along, Ginger sent his helper out to gather firewood. His helper was a slow-witted man named Horace Jinks, but the playful cowboys quickly dubbed him Horse. Firewood was scarce on the range, and if Horse missed a piece, Ginger whipped off his derby and gave him a hard rap that sent him scurrying after the deadfall. Rarely did they come across a thicket that filled the cowhide cooney slung under the wagon. Some days they found nothing, and Horse collected dried cow flops to burn as "prairie coal."

When we reached camp each evening, Ginger had supper going over a small fire of mesquite, and a half-dozen branding irons would be heating in another fire. We roped and branded cattle until nightfall, ate a quick supper, and fell wearily into our blanket rolls.

Most of the time it was more of a cow hunt than a roundup. The steers bunched around the water holes, and all you had to do was get them moving in the right direction. If a steer was mired in the mud, you were in for a long fight winching it out with ropes wrapped around saddle horns.

Still, enough cows wandered into the deep arroyos to keep us busy day after day rooting them out. A longhorn is an ornery, obstinate critter, and if a cowboy is foolish enough to give one a choice of directions, it's going to run the wrong way every time. One hot, dusty day I was urging a young bull up the steep banks of an arroyo when it suddenly reversed itself. The tip of one long horn swung wickedly in my direction. It would have gutted me had I not leaped from my buckskin and tumbled down to the bottom of the arroyo. I lost a little dignity, but I came out unscratched.

Sometimes I worked alone. Sometimes I worked with Chago Duran, a bronzed young Mexican in tight black pants and a high-crowned sombrero. He was a slight, mustachioed man with enough Indian blood to broaden his features and enough Spanish blood to give him an ample supply of touchy, Castilian pride. If he took to you, you could not ask for a truer friend. I reckon he could just about outride, outrope, and outshoot any man I'd ever run across.

Sometimes I worked with Alamo Rehnquist, a short, sinewy man who rode a horse like an extension of the animal. He was an open, friendly man and utterly fearless. He stood no higher than Major Mosby had, and like the Ranger leader he would charge any man or beast if he was provoked enough.

And sometimes I rode with Dusty Morgan, a whelp just barely weaned from his mother's teat. His adolescent voice still occasionally cracked, especially when he was excited. Dusty was too young to know fear. He was also too young to know when the smartest thing a man could do was back off. He reminded me of myself at that age.

Once and only once, I rode the range with Ed Crayler. Crayler was one of Angus's top hands. He was a man with one squint eye, yellow teeth, rancid breath, and a disposition to match. The short of it was that Crayler was a braggart and a coward.

Around the camp fire Crayler taunted Dusty and Zack Freeman, a former slave who worked as a wrangler and kept the remuda.

Every pound of coffee in the chuck wagon was packed with a peppermint stick. Ginger used the candy to reward whatever cowboy was in his favor at the moment, though in fact Ginger rarely looked upon any of the cowboys with anything less than contempt. But as it happened, the candy frequently went to Dusty. It never went to Crayler. Sometimes nobody got it.

Crayler suspected that Ginger was feeding the candy to his dog, Caesar. It stuck in his craw like a piece of meat that wouldn't go down. He didn't dare take it out directly on Ginger, so Dusty became the target.

He picked on Zack because Zack was black and a former slave, and thus, in Crayler's eyes, defenseless. I guess Crayler figured if Zack ever did fight back, the other cowhands would resent it and come to his aid.

The day I rode with Crayler, he decided to see how far he could push me. I think he took me for a fancy-pants lawyer riding along on some kind of lark. I didn't pay him much mind, and he got bolder by the hour. I wasn't looking for trouble, but I was only going to be pushed so far.

In the late afternoon he went too far.

His horse "accidentally" bumped against mine on the edge of an arroyo. I nearly went over the side, and only the surefootedness of my buckskin saved me from a nasty spill.

I leaped out of my saddle onto Crayler's back and pulled him to the ground. There I proceeded to pound the stuffing out of him.

He steered clear of me after that.

So I put the miles between Crayler and me and flushed out more strays until I knew I had to return to my office to tend to business.

I was also anxious to get back to Abby. Those long, lonely nights, I climbed into my blanket roll, stared at the bright prairie stars, and thought of little else.

As the roundup drew to a close, my share of dogies due me under my agreement with Angus was enough to fill my corral. I took only twenty back with me. My land was already taxed by the small herd I had accumulated last year, and I didn't have a dime to spare for grain or hay.

Dusty volunteered to help me drive the calves in, not that twenty calves were that much trouble. When I saw his face light up at the sight of Abby, I knew the real reason he had come.

I hung back and let him drive the calves into the corral. Dusty waved his riata furiously over his head and whistled shrilly. His batwing *aparejos* flapped in the wind as he spun his horse to head off an escaping calf. Dusty turned it into a grand show that Abby enjoyed immensely.

Abby applauded his horsemanship, and I thought Dusty's grin would split his face in two. He stammered and reddened every time she spoke to him or looked in his direction. "Shucks, ma'am" seemed to be the only words in his vocabulary. I never saw a happier kid than when she sent him away with his stomach straining from his fill of blackberry pie and his cheeks glowing from her chaste peck.

"I want a son just like that," she announced as we watched Dusty ride away.

"He's a good lad," I agreed. "Reminds me of myself when I was his age. The range will toughen him fast."

"But it won't take the gentleness out of him," she said. "Just as it hasn't taken it out of you."

I thought no more about it until darkness closed upon us. Despite the early spring, it still felt good to stand by a fire. I poked the embers to revive the flames. Abby took off her apron, wiped her hands on it before hanging it on a peg, and came to stand by me. I slipped an arm around her waist, and she leaned her head against my shoulders.

"You remember I said I wanted a son like Dusty," she whispered.

I nodded absently.

"Or maybe a son like you when you were a boy." She was silent for a long moment. The fire popped and hissed. The feel of her was soft and warm.

"Of course," she added, "it could be a girl."

I spun her around and held her by the shoulders. I opened my mouth, but no words came out.

She laughed gently and said, "You've been gone six weeks. A lot can happen in that time. I was almost sure the day you rode off, but I wanted Doc Sideley—"

"You saw Doc? What'd he say?"

She looked at me with that Madonna look of hers. "He said—" She hesitated. "He said I'm in the family way."

I threw my arms around her and hugged her tightly. Suddenly I released her. "I'm sorry," I stammered as awkwardly as Dusty. "I shouldn't hug you like that. It might hurt the baby. Our son."

I've always been one to keep my emotions to myself. I never wanted to burden other people with my troubles, and I've always felt my joys were too special to be shared. Until I met Abby. She allowed me to shamelessly express the feelings I'd always hidden from others. Right then and there I let out a "Whoopeee!" that would have commanded attention in the noisiest cow town saloon.

Abby laughed at my unexpected display, but her eyes glistened with moisture in the firelight.

Chapter Eight

The next morning I hitched up the buckboard, and Abby and I rode into San Miguel. She wanted to shop and visit, but she also tucked a broom and some rags into the back of the buckboard to tidy up my long-neglected office.

I tied up by the Stockman's Bank. We crossed the creaking wooden sidewalk into the bank. There was an outside entrance to my second-floor office—I didn't want my clients subjected to Otis Rankin's scrutiny—but I wanted to see if Otis had any work for me.

Otis welcomed me back and greeted Abby in his courtly manner. He said, "I 'spect, Miz Wheeler, you must be right proud to have your man back." A big smile crossed his broad, red face, and for once he didn't have a cigar stuck in the middle of it. Then he turned to me. "Ben, it's been a spell. I got a pile of stuff right here on my desk waiting for you."

Eyeing the broom and rags in Abby's hands, Otis said, "I guess we got us a spot of cleaning to do. Henry sweeps out after closing, but I don't 'spect he's been upstairs since you left."

The bank was a dark and solemn place, and its two occupants, Otis Rankin and Axel Swensen, added little humor to it. Otis looked upon banking as a sacred trust, and he tended to be a little pompous when doing business. Swensen was a pale and morose man. He never seemed to talk except when it was absolutely necessary, and even then he issued his words like the bank's hard-earned currency. He was the bank's bookkeeper and teller, and he was totally devoted in his service to Otis.

Two teller's cages faced the front door, and an ornate wooden balustrade separated the back of the bank. Otis opened the gate and stood back for Abby and me to pass through. In the rear was Otis's desk, an old leather couch, and a huge, squat vault with its heavy door slightly ajar. Otis usually worked at the desk, but if more than a few customers were waiting for Swensen, he would open the other teller's cage for a few minutes.

Otis picked up a bundle of papers from his desk and put them into my hands.

"I'll take care of these things first," I said.

"I'd 'preciate it, Ben. Some of 'em been waiting a spell."

The door to the stairs was between Otis's desk and the vault. Abby and I climbed the steep steps in the dim light. At the landing at the top, I found the key to my office and opened the door.

Abby stepped in ahead of me. Wrinkling her nose, she said, "It's so musty in here."

I dropped the documents onto the desk top, then rubbed a finger across the surface. I traced my Running W brand in the dust.

"If you spent more time tending to business in your own office and less time riding roundup for Angus Finlay, it might look more presentable," she said.

I threw her a glance, and her quick smile told me she was teasing. Working the range was hard, dusty, sweaty, tiring work, but those days on the plains filled me with a sense of freedom I hated to surrender.

Abby set to work with her broom and rags. I walked to the front windows and said, "Let's get some air in here. Place smells like Ginger's dog on a rainy day."

I opened a window and looked down on the rutted main street of San Miguel. If I had been of a demonstrative nature, I would have been tempted to shout my joy to the townspeople below: *"Come Thanksgiving I'm going to be a father!"* Across from the bank I spied Asa Stanley loading sacks of flour onto the back of a wagon in front of his general store. *"Hey, Asa, guess what? I'm going to be a father!"* I laughed at my own foolishness. Asa had seven children, and he might wonder why anyone would get excited over a minor thing like a pregnancy.

I couldn't see the street directly below me because the bank's flat porch roof extended out to the edge of the wooden sidewalk. I could see the Bluebonnet Saloon down the street, and even at this early hour it was doing a good business. A cowboy reeled out of the swinging front doors and nearly collided with a stout woman headed for Mrs. Barber's dress shop. He lifted his sweat-stained Stetson to her, but she twirled her parasol to put him out of sight and flounced off.

In front of the livery stables, Nimrod Jones's oldest boy, Albert, groomed a big roan. The barn was a dull red, and I doubted that Nimrod had painted it since that first coat a decade ago. The stables hid the blacksmith shop next to it, but I could hear a ring of steel that told me Bob Dudley was working on a wagon wheel.

I started to turn away when my eye was caught by a movement at the end of the street, where three new buildings had been slapped together and the bare pine boards were turning to ocher in the sun.

Four men rode slowly into town. They could be cowboys from an outlying ranch, coming to town after the roundup to spend their thirty dollars a month on a few trinkets and the raw whiskey Solomon Grace served at the bar of the Bluebonnet Saloon.

Yet the coating of alkali dust on their wrinkled linen dusters and the weary way they sat in the saddle told me they had ridden a long trail.

The sight of them gave me an uneasy feeling. They were too tense and watchful. They looked vaguely familiar, particularly the big man with a bushy black beard and the tall, clean-shaven man riding beside him.

I had to remind myself I didn't wear a badge anymore. As a former peace officer, I thought any stranger in town looked suspicious. But I was a lawyer now, and I had hung up my Colt .45. The only time I strapped it on nowadays was to pop at rattlers on roundup.

"There!" Abby said triumphantly. I turned from the window to admire her standing with a rag in her hand. She was a picture.

"Now it won't shame me to have you receive your clients."

I laughed. "Not too many of them breaking down the door to get in here. But it does look a sight better."

"Well, just you wait, Mr. Lawyer. Your reputation has already spread from the Pecos to the Colorado. I'm thinking it won't be long before they'll know your name in Austin."

"Next think you know you'll have me standing for the legislature," I said, shaking my head.

"Now, that's a thought, Mr. Wheeler. That truly is a thought."

I knew Abby better than to believe she was just chatting idly. If she had set her bonnet for Austin— But I didn't want to think about that. Not yet. I was still just a poor country lawyer.

I said, "You better scat. You got shopping and visiting to do, and I got these papers to take care of before Otis comes huffing and puffing up the stairs to see what's taking so long."

I cupped her under the chin, raised her face to me, and kissed her. She smelled lightly of lilac.

"I better run," she said.

"I'll see you down the steps."

"Darling," she said firmly, "I'm only pregnant, not helpless."

"The steps are kind of steep."

"I'll walk slowly," she said.

I watched her careful descent for a moment, then called after her, "I hope you spend just as slowly. A dollar is hard to come by."

I heard the trill of her laughter as I turned back to my desk. The swivel chair squeaked in protest under my weight. Why hadn't I remembered the oil? Creaking saddle leather was a song to my ears, but this could drive me to distraction.

I picked up the batch of mortgages and liens Otis had handed me in the bank just as I heard the sound from the bank below.

CRACK!

I knew instinctively it was a .45.

Cold fear clutched my heart.

CRACK!

The second shot sounded before I could even rise from my desk.

The four men I had seen riding into town! Why hadn't I acted on my suspicions?

My throat suddenly felt as dry as an alkali flat. I couldn't swallow. My hands began to sweat.

Abby was down in the bank!

Chapter Nine

I wanted to run down the stairs and see if Abby was safe. But I was unarmed and knew I'd be looking down the barrels of four guns. I prayed she was unharmed.

I tore off my coat—my black lawyer's coat, Abby called it—and let it fall to the floor as I raced to the front window. I climbed out onto the porch roof. I could see the rumps of their horses tied to the hitching rail in front of the bank.

I peered over the roof's edge. One man stood nervously by the horses. He had a scattergun in his hands. He couldn't see me because of the broad brim of his hat. I prayed that he didn't look up.

I could see the fringes of a reddish beard under the hat. His ample stomach pressed against the duster. What I could see of his fancy clothes beneath the duster told me this dude was probably more comfortable in a saloon dealing aces from the bottom of a deck than robbing banks.

The heavy tread of boots on the wooden sidewalk below frustrated my decision to jump the man. Several shots exploded beneath me. A bullet splintered through the roof only inches from my right boot.

A woman screamed somewhere down the street. A dog barked. Doors slammed shut. Wild shouting came from all sides.

The horses whinnied nervously and stirrup straps and saddles creaked under the weight of mounting riders. I remained motionless, not wanting any sound to betray my presence until I was ready to make my move.

I knew all four men were in the saddle. I caught glimpses of them and could see the dust rising as the horses pranced about. I could hear the leather and the stamping hooves.

"What'd you have to go and shoot for, you dumb Arkie?" said a voice below me.

"How'n hell was I supposed to know it was a woman?" answered a high-pitched voice. "Suppose it had been the sheriff, tell me what then?"

"What's done is done," said another voice.

They shot a woman! The words left me utterly empty. For a moment I seemed almost oblivious to the action swirling on the street below me. Never before had I felt such cold hatred or been compelled to such recklessness.

The Arkie shot a woman in the bank! *Abby was the only woman in the bank!*

I stepped to the edge of the roof. I didn't know which was the Arkie who had pulled the trigger. I did know it wasn't the fat man. But it didn't matter. I was going to kill them all. With my bare hands, if necessary!

The four horses circled aimlessly below me as the riders blasted away at any townsman foolish enough to show his head. They moved in a cloud of gun smoke. The acrid smell of black powder stung my nostrils.

The fat man who had held the horses came beneath me. I braced myself for the leap. But another horse, frightened by the noise and commotion, bolted suddenly to the right and butted the fat man's horse out of the way.

I was in midair when the new horse and rider came under me. Before I hit I heard the big man with the black beard bellow: "Let's ride, you sonsabitches!"

I reached down with both hands and grabbed the rider's shoulders and drew myself toward him. My rump landed just behind the cantle of his saddle. The thick blanket roll tied behind the cantle cushioned my landing. Still, the force of the impact sent air rushing out of my lungs in a whoosh.

The horse kicked up its hind legs in protest. I held on tightly. I had no intention of being bucked off.

"Wha' th' hell!" the rider cursed in surprise. For an instant he wasn't sure what had hit him.

I wrapped one arm tightly around his waist, and with the other reached for his pistol. I didn't succeed, but I got an iron grip on his right wrist. It kept him from twisting the gun around to shoot me.

"Git this critter offen my back!" he screamed. He cocked his head around to see what had hold of him. His mouth was twisted in rage and his dark eyes were wild.

I knew that face! I knew that man! I struggled to put a name to that face.

I clung tightly to the rider to make them think twice before throwing lead at me. At the same time I dug my heels into his horse's flanks. It caused his horse to jump and kick and prance around, forcing the others to keep their distance.

As we whirled around, the other three riders flashed by. I got my first good look at the big man with the black beard. He had a hawk nose a Comanche chief would envy. Suddenly I recognized him.

Bill Smoot! I'd had trouble with him in Kansas four years ago. He'd robbed the bank at Colchester.

Now I knew the man I was clinging to—*Montana Smith!* A back-shooter and Smoot's cohort in half a dozen escapades in Kansas. He'd killed a man from ambush in Dodge.

I nearly brought the two of them to tree on the banks of the Arkansas one wintry night a week after the bank robbery. A sudden blizzard swept down across the prairie, and this was the first time I'd seen them since.

The fat man flashed by. I couldn't find a name, but I'd seen a hundred tinhorns like him working keno and dealing poker in cow town saloons.

The fourth man, then, was the Arkie!

The twisting horse quickly brought him into my line of sight. He was a baby-faced kid! My God, it could have been Dusty Morgan! Then I saw the eyes. They were like the icy blue pits of hell. The dead eyes of a killer. I had seen eyes like that before. Men with eyes like that killed for the sport of it.

The Arkie brought up his gun, and a tight little smile crossed his baby lips. "This is th' day y'meet yore Maker!" he sneered.

I hugged Montana tighter than a Beau Brummell sparking in a buggy. Suddenly I realized: the kid didn't care if he hit Montana or not. Maybe they had quarreled in camp. Maybe he figured it was just one less man to take a share of the loot. More likely, he just didn't give a damn and was licking his chops over carving another notch on his long-barreled .45.

It was aimed straight at me. I looked right into the black hole of the bore. His thumb pulled back the hammer and his finger tightened on the trigger. His eyes told me he wanted to kill me.

"Damn you, Bayliss!" The booming shout came from behind me. It was Smoot.

"You hit Montana and I'll make sure it yore las' day on earth!"

I saw Bayliss ease off the trigger. His lips curled into another cruel smile, and he snarled, "Damned if this ain't yore lucky day, Texican!"

He had hardly uttered the last word when the back of my head exploded. My eyes went out of focus. I loosened my grip on Montana, and he elbowed me off the back of his horse.

As I hit the ground, my head jerked sharply. Through bleary eyes I could see that Smoot had come up behind me and hit me with the butt end of his gun. My attention had been on the Arkie.

I rolled in the dusty street, trying to avoid the horses' hooves digging holes in the dirt just inches from my face. I kept moving. I didn't want to give the Arkie—or anyone else—a clear shot.

In front of the bank, Otis Rankin stood like an enraged guardian. He had a big Peacemaker in his hand, and he knew how to use it. It was a snub-nosed Shopkeeper's Model. He fired twice, and the gun belched smoke and fire.

The men were dodging bullets, yet Bayliss reined his horse, twisted in the saddle, and took aim at me over his shoulder. The bullet kicked dust in my face. He didn't have time for a second shot. Otis sent a round that tore a neat little hole in the brim of his sweat-streaked hat.

"Ride, dammit, ride!" Smoot shouted above the bedlam.

The four horsemen fought for control of their frightened animals. Several raced in circles before all of them beat a path for the town's edge. Not more than two dozen buildings lined San Miguel's main street. It wouldn't take them long to be in the plains.

I was on my feet. Without a word I took Otis' pistol. He released it willingly.

I stepped to the middle of the street and took careful aim at the fleeing riders. I wanted the Arkie, but with their backs to me, and at that distance, I couldn't be sure.

I picked a back at random and fired. The .45 kicked in my hand and a halo of flame and smoke flashed at the end of the barrel. Automatically my thumb cocked the weapon, and I pulled the trigger again. All I heard was a click.

Otis clapped me on the back. "You got one!" he said excitedly. "He nearly fell off his horse! You put a hole right between the shoulder blades."

Suddenly, as though he remembered something, the excitement left him and his face paled. I didn't want to ask him what he had remembered. Not yet.

The departure of the desperadoes brought the townspeople flooding into the street. They gathered in animated little groups and looked helplessly at the dust cloud left by the fleeing riders.

"Asa," I called, and the sturdy storekeeper turned his attention to me. "We'll need a posse. See what you can do about horses and men."

He set immediately to recruiting men, and I saw no lack of volunteers as I hailed Albert.

The stable boy ran eagerly to me. "Take a horse," I instructed, "and ride as fast as you can to the Lazy A. Tell Angus we need as many men as he can spare. Tell him to meet us at Three Mile Junction."

I could no longer postpone the painful question nagging at my mind. I looked at Otis. He avoided my pleading eyes.

All I could utter was a single word: *"Abby?"*

I could see that Otis, too, dreaded this moment. He started to speak. He swallowed hard. I knew the answer written on his sad face.

"Ben," he said, then hesitated for an eternity. "I'm sorry."

Otis quickly told me what had happened.

Three of the bandits had entered the bank. The fat, red-bearded man stayed outside with the horses. There were no customers in the bank at the time.

"Stand easy, gents, and no one's gonna get hurt," said the big man with the black beard, the man I recognized as Bill Smoot.

The men had their guns out, and after Smoot's warning hardly another word was spoken.

The tall, clean-shaven man stood by the door. That was Montana.

Smoot pushed past Otis, kicked open the gate, and unfolded a sack as he headed for the open vault.

Smoot pulled the heavy door open all the way, then squatted in front of the vault. He immediately began raking the packets of money into the sack. Normally Otis never kept more money in the bank than was needed for everyday business. On this day, however, he had extra cash to meet the big ranch payrolls. Slightly more than six thousand dollars was in the vault.

Out of the corner of his eyes, Otis spied Swensen edge his right hand toward the teller's cage drawer. Otis kept a loaded .45 in that drawer. At that moment, however, he prayed the Swede would come up empty-handed.

The kid, the Arkie I heard called Bayliss, saw Swensen's furtive movement.

The pistol he had aimed at Otis swung in a gunmetal blur and exploded like a thunderclap. Swensen's hand never reached the drawer. He was dead before he hit the floor.

Smoot jumped like a jackrabbit, spilling dollar bills on the floor.

At that same instant the staircase door by the safe opened.

Abby stood in the doorway at the bottom of the steps. Her right hand started toward her mouth. A scream formed in her throat.

Before her hand reached her bosom, Bayliss's gun exploded again. The impact threw Abby back into the stairwell. She was dead before she had fully grasped what was happening.

"Sweet Mother a God!" Smoot swore. "Now y'tore it!"

The fat man opened the door by Montana and looked in nervously. "That shootin'—" He saw the two bodies, and the words froze in his mouth. The color drained from his ruddy face. "Jesus!" he finally sputtered, "I knew that Arkie was gonna be trouble! He kilt a woman!"

Bayliss didn't even bother to look at the fat man. He hissed, "And I knowed you was too yeller to even watch th' horses."

"Things is gettin' awful edgy out there," the tinhorn croaked in a voice that cracked like an adolescent's. "We better skedaddle!"

"Not till we git what we came fer," said Bayliss.

Smoot, scooping up the last of the money from the safe, was getting very agitated. "Git back outside!" he ordered the tinhorn. "We can't have nobody layin' an ambush for us!"

Bayliss holstered his pistol and cleaned out the teller cash drawer. He dumped the money into the sack. He picked up the big Colt in the drawer and shoved it under his gunbelt. Then he leveled his icy blue eyes on Otis. His gun was in his hand again. He said to Smoot, "What about him? We don't want no witnesses."

Smoot, tying a leather thong around the open end of the sack, said, "Boy, you ain't got a lick a sense!"

I knew the rest of the story. That's where I came in. I also knew that Otis kept another gun in his desk drawer.

Otis tried to persuade me not to go into the bank, but I wouldn't be stopped. Several women were tending to Abby and had removed her to the old leather couch by Otis's desk. They stepped aside silently as I approached.

A blanket had been stretched over her. I pulled it down to reveal her face. She appeared to be in tranquil sleep. A wisp of hair was on her forehead.

I knelt by the couch and looked at her face. How I wanted to wake her from that sleep! I kissed her forehead and her cool, still lips.

As I said a silent prayer for Abby and the child we would never have, a tear drop fell on the collar of her dress.

Chapter Ten

Night was falling fast, and the scant tracks were growing more difficult to read in the fading light. The trail led almost due east from San Miguel.

We had been following the signs since the four men had robbed the Stockman's Bank at midmorning. Hours of scanning the dusty road before it disappeared into hardpan had trained my eyes to distinguish the shoes of each horse.

We rode slowly as I leaned from the saddle to peer carefully at the ground. Sometimes it was only a few pebbles pressed into the soil. Once or twice the ground softened enough so that I could see the clear bite of a shoe.

I nodded to Angus, who rode just behind me at the head of the hastily assembled posse of townspeople and cowhands. Pointing down, I said, "They were still riding at a good clip when these tracks were made. The front of the shoes dug in pretty deep."

Angus shifted in the saddle and squinted his eyes for a clearer view. He removed his hat and wiped his sweaty brow with his bandanna. "Aye," he said. "They can't keep it up much longer. They've got to rest their horses soon."

I looked back at the sun. It was a dull red ball plunging behind the low, eroded foothills behind us. Our shadows stretched out on the trail. After a few minutes they began to fade and disappear. The western sky turned orange, then purple, and dusk was upon us.

With sundown, a breeze freshened across the plain. It began to dry our sweat-soaked shirts. I turned my face this way and that until the fresh air felt the coolest. The wind was coming from the east, just a few points to the south. It smelled of bluebonnets and sun-cooked grass. I had hoped for the smell of horseflesh, or fresh-dropped manure, or even the pungent smell of smoke, but I was disappointed.

"Why don't we rest for a spell," Angus suggested.

With only a nod, I stepped down from my horse, a dappled gray I had borrowed from Nimrod Jones's stable. Six men had ridden from town with me. They were hastily armed with whatever weapons they could collect.

I carried a Peacemaker and a belt and holster that Asa Stanley had snatched from a display counter in his store. It was a Colt Single Action Army Revolver, the Cavalry Model with a seven-and-a-half-inch barrel. It was one of the new pistols that used a metal cartridge. A Winchester was in the saddle boot.

Otis had wanted to ride with us, but I had persuaded him that his place was at the bank.

Angus, with eight more men, had joined us east of Three Mile Junction. I was happy to see that he had Chago with him. I'd feel safe charging a Cheyenne war party if I knew Chago was at my side. He was the kind of man I welcomed as a friend and would dread as an enemy. I was less happy to see Crayler, but I figured he was probably handy with a gun. If we met up with Smoot's bunch, we'd need men with a keen eye and a steady hand.

The weary men squatted by their horses. There was no wood for a fire, so we drank warm water from our canteens and chewed on jerky and dry biscuits. Several men opened sacks of tobacco and rolled quirleys.

Angus sat on the ground beside me and pulled at his long sandy mustache. "I brought a lantern or two," he said. "We could light up and follow the trail some more."

I had an unlit cheroot in my mouth. Out of the side of my mouth I said, "They'd spot a light ten miles off. No sense tipping our hand sooner'n we have to."

"Aye," Angus agreed, taking another tug at his mustache. After a moment, he said, "We could ride blind and trust to luck they keep on going in the same direction."

"That's what I been thinking. They got to roost sometime."

Chago sat beside us on the hard ground. He put his sombrero on one raised knee and sipped at his canteen. "Ees funny," he said. "Thees taste just like *agua*. I thought I filled my *botella* with tequila. But ees okay. I forget the lime, too."

He grinned broadly. "*El jefe* say we ride in the dark. The moon she be up in another two, three hours. She not a full moon, but if your gringo eyes fail you, Chago can see fine in the dark."

Angus grunted. "The thing for you to do, my boy, is see that you don't smile too much. Those pearly whites of yours shine like the lighthouse at Oban. They make a tempting target, moon or no moon."

It was the first laugh we'd had on the long ride. My mind had been on one thing, and the tension had left me stiff-necked and headachy. It was good to relax.

We were all tense, and none of us wanted to speak of the morning's tragedy. I sensed that it was a tacit agreement among them. Even Angus, who loved Abby like a daughter, had not mentioned it after a few choked words of condolence when he joined us.

A number of times I had seen Dusty Morgan chewing on his lower lip and blinking eyes reddened from crying. Several times he wiped his nose on his sleeve. Each of us was wrapped in his private grief, and no one took notice. Angus had not wanted to bring a boy as young as Dusty, but the lad would not be left behind. He had a schoolboy crush on Abby, and I suspected he would have dispatched her killers with less remorse than any of us.

Even Ed Crayler's conduct had been beyond reproach, for once. He had not uttered a word of ridicule to Dusty, and he kept his peace with Chago. He proved to be a valuable man in helping me track. Nevertheless I could not suppress the feeling that like all bullies he was anxious to tangle with the desperadoes only in a one-sided fight.

I put a match to the cheroot. It was a habit I had picked up during long, lonely nights of vigil while a lawman. I smoked the strong cigar in silence, lost in my thoughts and grief.

Presently Angus said, "There's a line shack about four, five miles from here."

"We be there by the time the moon ees up," Chago added.

"East of here?" I asked.

"They keep on steady they can't miss it," Angus said.

"I have spent many a winter night in eet," said Chago. "A weary traveler find eet hard to pass by. Especially eef such an *hombre* ees burdened by the additional weight of your bullet."

"You ever decide which one you hit?" Angus asked.

"No," I said, snuffing out the cigar in the dirt. "But I aim to find out right soon. If it's not the Arkie, I've got a bullet for him, too. His life ain't worth a plugged nickel."

I stood up and put my hat on. Even in the dark I knew Angus's eyes were fixed on me.

"I want Bayliss in my gun sights," I said angrily. "I'll give him the same chance he gave Abby. No, I'll do better'n that. I'll give him an even chance, which is more'n he gave Abby. He shot her down in cold blood. I'm going to kill him, Angus. I'm going to make it *real* personal. And then I'm going to take care of Smoot and Montana and the tinhorn. As far as I'm concerned, they all had a hand in it, too."

It was the first time I had expressed the terrible thoughts that had been smoldering within me since morning. I wanted *revenge*! I knew it wouldn't bring Abby back. I knew it wouldn't even make me feel better. Still, I was driven to it. I knew Angus would counsel against it. I knew Moses would, too, if he were still alive. And I knew Abby would—I broke off the thought and said more harshly than I intended, "Let's find that line shack of yours, Angus! We got unfinished business!"

Chapter Eleven

The air was clear and cool. I was grateful for the sheepskin coat Angus had brought for me. I had left town only in my shirtsleeves.

I searched the cloudless sky and quickly located the North Star. To the west and slightly above it, the Big Dipper hung downward. I placed the time approximately at ten o'clock.

"The moon she's coming up," Chago said in a low voice behind me.

The moon was only a sliver on the horizon ahead of us. As it climbed into the night sky, the silver grew larger until it became a luminous pewter plate with a nick out of one side. It cast a dim glow over the land. The riders behind me were gray and shadowy.

For the last hour we had been climbing a rise. Now it gave way to country broken by shallow arroyos and an occasional stand of cottonwood trees clinging to the water's edge. Some areas were thick with creosote bush and yucca.

Angus spurred his horse to catch up with me. We hadn't spoken since sundown. He had spent most of the time riding at the rear. I guess we were both mulling over what I had said.

"We're almost there," he said as he drew beside me. "The shack's on the other side of the next arroyo. I built it up above the flood waters, yet close enough so a man's got fresh water at his doorstep."

"How far you reckon to the arroyo?"

"Hundred yards. Maybe two. Pray it's the next arroyo, 'cause I've already said as much and the boy'll think I'm losing me touch if it ain't."

"Too bad you're not a betting man, Angus."

I had thought Angus was brooding over my vow of vengeance, but if he was, he didn't show it now. Angus was a hard man, and if he got his back up he could be as righteous as a biblical patriarch. Yet I doubted that Angus had the heart to track a man down and shoot him.

"The shack's close," Angus said. "I can feel it in my bones."

We had been riding slow, and now we reined in.

"We'd better go the rest of the way by foot," I said, stepping down from my horse.

Chago moved close behind me and said into my ear, "*Señor*, my nose has never lied to me. Do you not smell smoke?"

I sniffed the air. It was very faint, but I caught a whiff of it. Like the smell of a dying fire. Then a fresh waft of air brought another odor and my mouth watered involuntarily. *Bacon!* "Somebody's been frying bacon," I said.

Angus alighted from his big bay and said in a low voice, "Somebody's in the line shack—that's for sure. I don't have to ask who that somebody is."

All the riders dismounted, and Angus drew them into a tight circle so that we could discuss our tactics. We still couldn't see the shack, even with the three-quarter moon high in the sky. There was a slight rise before the edge of the arroyo, which kept the shack from view.

"Keep your voices low and keep the horses quiet," I said.

"If you got spurs or anything else that's likely to jingle, take 'em off," Angus added.

"The desperadoes are sure to have a guard posted," I said. "I don't want to take any chance of scaring them off. We're going to go in nice 'n' quiet."

Angus said, "Most of you men know this area. I built that shack with my own two hands in 'fifty-seven. It's just one room, a fireplace, a couple of bunks, and not enough furniture to spit at. I built it out of limestone, except the roof, so you can pepper away at it till doomsday and you ain't gonna put a dent in it. It's a little fortress. On the south side's a lean-to for the horses.

"There's a door and two windows facing the creek. That's where she's vulnerable. That's where we'll have to hit 'em. Them two's the only windows. They got wooden shutters covering 'em, but that won't stop a bullet. If we catch 'em in the shack from the front, there ain't no way on God's green earth they can get out unless they start digging."

"What's the layout around the shack?" I asked. In all the time I had ridden for Angus, I had never been here.

Angus pointed toward the east. "The arroyo's about a hundred yards thataway. You can't see it from here 'cause the ground rises a bit before the bluff. There's a little creek runs through the arroyo. I 'spect this time of year it's probably got no more'n a foot of water in it. When the skies open up, it can be a real gullywasher. The bluff on this side is about ten, twelve feet high. It's pretty steep, so watch yourself going down. The other side of the arroyo is pretty well eroded. It's no climb atall. More slope than bluff. Shack's no more'n twenty feet from the top. On the north side's a stand of cottonwood trees. They run in a straight line from the creek to well past the shack. Planted 'em myself as a windbreak."

I digested the information, then said, "The way I see it we gotta hit 'em hard and we gotta hit 'em fast. If you take 'em by surprise, they'll be confused and scared."

"What you got in mind, Ben?" Angus asked.

"I think we should split into three groups and box 'em in. We'll throw our main effort against the front, where the door and windows are. We got sixteen men. I say half hit the front. The rest we split evenly, four and four, and cover the flanks."

I looked around. Everyone nodded in agreement. "Sounds good to me," said one man.

Chago smiled and said, "Benito Juarez himself would approve of such a plan."

I looked at Angus. "Aye," he agreed. "We'll have them in an enfilade. That's the kind of tactic they teach at Sandhurst. That's the way Hannibal nipped the Romans at Cannae. If only we had a few of the African's elephants."

"Okay," I said, "Angus and I will lead the main force against the front of the shack." I turned to Ed Crayler. "Ed, you take three men and set up the south flank."

"Ain't nobody gonna get by me," Crayler bragged. He fingered the handle of the long-barreled Remington .44 in his worn holster. Crayler was a blustering bully, and in all the time I had known him I had never seen him pick on a man unless he was dead certain he could take him or cow him down. I was taking a chance, but now was the time to see if he could back up his words with action.

"I'm counting on that," I said. "You better stay back from the shack. That'll keep you out of our line of fire. Be a good idea, too, if you post the men in a line from the front of the shack to the—"

"I been in tight fixes before," Crayler interrupted.

Angus said sharply, "You'll be in another if you don't listen to Ben and take heed!"

Crayler, momentarily taken aback, fell silent.

I continued. "If they've got a guard, it's a pretty good bet he's going to be in the lean-to stable. Keep a close watch. The other thing you gotta look for is that they don't make a break for their horses."

"Where you want 'em shot, head, chest, or legs?" said Crayler. Obviously his bravado had returned. Several men laughed.

I turned to Chago. "Chago, you take the north flank. Take your horses and walk them about two hundred yards upstream. Cross over and come in behind the windbreak. Stay hidden behind the cottonwoods. I don't want you to do any shooting. Just be ready to ride in case they somehow get away."

Chago's marksmanship would be handy at my side, but I needed his horsemanship more in case everything fell apart.

I prayed that it wouldn't.

Chapter Twelve

We lay on our bellies, overlooking the rise at the edge of the arroyo. The moon was almost directly overhead. It was still unobscured, but heavy, dark clouds were building on the northern horizon. The shack lay before us across the divide, bathed in a soft, eerie glow.

"Awful quiet," said Angus.

"No light in the shack," I added. "Maybe they bedded down."

"Maybe so, but if I was a betting man I'd say they got a pair of eyes keeping watch."

The roof overhang cast a deep shadow, especially in the lean-to stable area. Where the moonlight reached the sides of the shack each individual stone was visible. If they were in there, four men could put up a hell of a fight. The stone walls were at least a foot thick. The only sign of life was an occasional spark that escaped from the chimney.

We slid back from the rise to move to a spot downstream where Angus said horses and cattle had beaten down the steep wall of the arroyo.

Suddenly, to our right, came a heavy fluttering sound. The sound grew louder as wings beat against the air to gain altitude.

"Damn!" I swore.

"Looks like we scared up a covey of quail in the grass," said Angus.

"They heard that for sure. Thank God no one got nervous enough to fire a round."

We slid down the crumbly, dusty side of the arroyo, breaking with our heels. The creek was not deep enough to wash over the tops of our boots.

The other side was like a ramp. We climbed just far enough up the slope so that we could rest our guns on the crest. The eight of us lined up along the edge. Close enough together so that we could concentrate our fire on the windows and doors. Far enough apart so that we didn't present a solid target.

Angus and I peered over the top. The shack was near enough to spit at.

There was no movement. Not a sound.

The door was shut and the solid wooden shutters on the two windows were buttoned up tight.

In our nostrils were the smells of smoke, grass, the cottonwoods, our own sweat, and the pungent, grassy odor of fresh horse manure.

After looking things over, I said to Angus, "You notice anything funny about the stable?"

Angus turned his attention to the shadowed lean-to along the south side of the shack. He squinted at it for the longest time. "Aye," he said finally. "I don't think they got any horses in there. I sure can't see any, and I sure can't hear any."

"They could have them staked out a piece for grazing." I suggested.

"Maybe so," he said, not fully convinced. "I hope they didn't hear them quail and fly the coop. Them birds set up a frightful racket." He sighed. "'The best laid schemes of mice and men.' Well, it's now or never. Are we ready? Is everyone in position yet?"

"I saw Crayler and his men creep in downstream a few minutes ago. I haven't caught sight of Chago yet."

"You know Chago as well as I do, Ben. You're not going to see him, but he's there. I think it's time to let our friends know we're here."

I raised myself slightly, and at the top of my voice I shouted, "You in the house! This is a posse from San Miguel! Throw down your weapons and come out with your hands up!"

I slunk back and waited.

I was answered by silence from the shack. The only sound was the rush of the wind across the rippling grass and swaying cottonwood trees. The breeze had stiffened as the storm clouds rolled in from the north.

"Give 'em another minute," Angus said. "Maybe they're talking it over."

After a minute, I repeated the warning.

We waited another few minutes, but there was still no response. Suddenly a townsman to my right rose up and started to scale the bank. "Hell," he said, "they done skedaddled."

The shutter of one window flew open with a bang. A ball of fire blossomed in the window.

CRACK!

The townsman grunted and stopped in his tracks. His arms flew up and he appeared to be carried backward by the impact. He tumbled down the slope and lay motionless at the bottom. We had no time to see who it was or go to his aid.

Every gun among us answered at once. The noise was deafening. The smell of gunpowder was choking. Bullets splintered the shutters and door. Chips of wood flew in all directions. Tiny dust clouds puffed up where lead struck the stone. Several shots ricocheted off with a whine.

Guns flashed to the right. Ed Crayler and his men fired furiously, although there was no target but the empty stable and the solid stone wall of the shack.

We kept up a steady fusillade, quickly emptying our guns, reloading and emptying them again.

Since that first shot from the cabin, not a bullet had been fired in our direction. My first thought was that we had driven them to cover. Then I began to wonder.

"Hold your fire!" I commanded. "Hold your fire!"

Several men popped off a few more rounds. Then there was silence.

Angus and I slid back down the slope to examine the man who had been shot. The initial shock of the bullet or the tumble down the bluff had apparently knocked him out. I had thought he was dead, but he was sitting up and pressing a handkerchief to his left shoulder. I saw that it was Dayton Pryor, the town's carpenter.

Angus knelt by the fallen man to examine the wound. I dipped a bandanna into the creek and handed it to Angus to wash away the blood.

I helped him remove Pryor's coat. Angus ripped away the left sleeve and looked at the wound in the bright moonlight. After a moment he said, "Leastways, we won't have to dig for a bullet. Went clean through like a whistle."

Pryor gasped in pain as Angus dabbed at the wound with the wet cloth. He wrapped the torn sleeve over Pryor's shoulder and under his arm for a makeshift bandage. "You're a lucky man, Dayton," Angus said. "If that bullet had killed you, who would build your coffin?"

Now that I knew the bank robbers hadn't claimed another victim, my mind was back on the shack. I suspected something was amiss, and I wanted to get it settled.

Dusty stood beside me. "What do we do now, Mr. Wheeler?"

"I think what we do now is find out who's in that shack."

"You can count on me," Dusty said eagerly. "This is just like them days when y'used to marshal, I'll bet. They ever put you in a dime novel, Mr. Wheeler? I got lots of 'em, but I ain't never seen none 'bout you."

Dusty frequently declared that he was seventeen. But as I examined his boyish face and slim figure in the moonlight I doubted he would reach that age before the next snowfall.

I said, "Dusty, I know I can count on you. That's why I want you to stay here and look after Mr. Pryor and make sure that no one escapes in this direction."

"You bet, Mr. Wheeler!" He took out his gun and examined the cylinder to see that it was loaded with caps and balls. The Remington .44, which his daddy had carried through the Civil War, was so big I wondered if he needed both hands to hold it steady. The gun had an eight-inch octagonal barrel and weighed just under three pounds.

As I turned to leave, I said, "I don't think you're gonna find any books about me, Dusty. I never met up with Mr. Ned Buntline."

I pulled Angus aside. "Something don't set right with me about that shack. I think it's time we went in and looked for ourselves."

"I got that same feeling," he said. "Somebody fires one shot, then nothing. Don't seem right—lessen we got him."

"Spread the word down the line. I want everybody to hold his fire. I'm going into the shack. You better send somebody up to let Chago know what's going on."

I climbed the embankment and ran in a low crouch toward Crayler.

I sang out first before making the dash. I didn't want any nasty surprises caused by an itchy trigger finger.

When I got to Crayler, I said, "I'm going into the shack. I could use a good man to back me up."

He grinned. "You know I'm game."

My worry was that Crayler was always game—until it got dangerous. I weighed the possibilities. If he bolted and ran, it could cost my life. I wished Alamo or Chago were nearby.

Unless I wanted to make an issue of it, it looked like I was stuck with Crayler.

"Things been mighty quiet for a spell," he said. "You figger they playin' possum?"

"I don't know. But let's find out."

We circled behind the shack, then closed in on the north side. I had my gun in my right hand. I touched the stone wall with my left hand as we crept around to the front. At the corner I stopped and stuck my head out cautiously to look around. I couldn't see anything, and I couldn't hear anything.

I slowly thumbed the hammer back on my Peacemaker until I heard it click. I had five shots in the cylinder. I never carry a round under the hammer. Only a fool would risk shooting himself in the foot.

I turned back to Crayler and put a finger to my lips for silence. He nodded his head. I motioned to him to follow me. I ducked around the corner, keeping close to the wall at the front of the shack.

I kept my pistol ready for anything. The wooden shutter on one of the windows was still open. In fact, it had been nearly blasted off its hinges. I pressed my face against the cold stones at the opening and peered in cautiously. It was a stygian darkness in the shack.

I crouched down below the window so that I would not be silhouetted against the moonlight, and crept to the door. I waited for Crayler to join me.

I pressed on the door. It held tight. The wooden bolt was probably in place inside. The door looked sturdy, but it was probably built only to stop the wind and snow and the occasional curious cow that might wander by. I prayed that Angus hadn't built it to withstand two strong and determined men.

I gestured to Crayler to put our shoulders to the door. He nodded that he understood and moved up beside me. We leaned back, and together we threw our weight against the door.

I heard it crack, but it held.

We both quickly drew back behind the safety of the rock, but no shots came splintering through the door.

On our second try, the door gave way with a crunching noise, and we stumbled inside.

CRACK!

A flash exploded low in a corner of the one-room shack.

I threw myself to the dirt floor. My eardrums rang from the gunshot in the confined space.

Two more shots blasted through the tiny shack.

At the same time I fired three more shots with lightning speed at the flashing gunbursts. The acrid smell of burned gunpowder filled the shack.

"Goddamn!" Crayler cried in the dark. "He hit me! The son of a bitch hit me! I'm bleeding! I got blood all over my face!"

"Shut up, you damned fool!" I said through clenched teeth.

I kept my gun aimed low at the corner. I had kept two bullets in reserve.

Slowly my eyes grew accustomed to the dark. Moonlight reflected dully in through the open window and door. I could make out an overturned chair. A table. I saw Crayler cowering in the corner.

At least I could make out a dark form on the floor in the corner.

I reached out and felt the toe of a boot pointed toward the ceiling. I curled my fingers around it and gave it a good yank. Nothing. I was pulling on dead weight.

I inched along past the feet. My gun was aimed at where I knew his chest was. I found his gunbelt. Then an arm and a gun in the hand. The barrel was still warm. I took the gun out of the hand, and the hand flopped back lifelessly.

I stood up and looked back at Crayler. I said, "You can get up now, gunslinger. The danger's over."

Without a word, he scrambled to his feet and fled out the door. He clutched his face with one hand.

At the door I called to Angus to bring up a lantern.

Angus lighted the kerosene lantern in the arroyo. It cast a bright yellow halo over the top of the rise. It bathed the front of the shack in light and illuminated the tops of the cottonwoods swaying relentlessly in the wind.

The wind had veered to the north and grew even stronger. Dark clouds scudded rapidly across the sky and hid the moon. I could smell rain in the air.

As the lantern was carried up the slope, the men gathered nervously in clusters. They were silhouetted against the yellow corona. Angus reached the top, and the men's faces were visible for the first time in hours. They looked haggard and anxious.

Angus was equally anxious. "Those shots—you all right? Crayler came running down like a scared rabbit."

"I think he got himself bloodied."

"Just a scratch. The bullet grazed his cheek and nicked his earlobe. He'll probably be bragging about it before the night's over. Whadda you got inside?"

"One dead man. Leastways, he's dead now. The others must have hightailed it before we got here."

He followed me in, and the rough interior of the shack was suddenly revealed in the stark light. Several men crowded at the door and others hung in the windows.

The dead man lay on his back, his head pushed up by the stone wall.

Angus held the light up high, and I stared down at the body.

His wild eyes stared lifelessly back at me. The same wild eyes I had seen that morning when I had leaped onto the back of his horse.

"Montana Smith," I said.

The information passed swiftly outside and was repeated by every lip.

Angus said, "His mortal soul has departed for the depths of hell."

A man pushed his way through the men for a closer look. "Montana Smith," he said. "I hear'd a him. Don't look so tough now."

Another said, "Jesse James hisself couldna stood up to th' lead we throwed in here."

Angus handed the light to one of his cowboys and knelt over the body. He opened the bloodstained buffalo coat, ripped open the woolen shirt, and exposed three bullet wounds in the chest.

"I heard six shots," Angus said.

"He fired three times, and so did I."

"I figured as much. You hit him with every shot."

Below the wounds was a cloth wrapped around his chest. Angus rolled the body over and peeled the coat and shirt up until he reached the cloth. It was soaked with blood.

"I guess that settles which one you shot in town," he said.

A cowhand asked, "Boss, you figger them others left him here to stall us while they made dust?"

Angus stood up. "Don't seem likely. That's a bad wound in the back. Likely his lungs filled with blood. Probably didn't have th' strength to ride anymore."

"I agree with Angus," I said. "Montana and Bill Smoot rode together for a long time. I ran into 'em a few times up in Kansas. They were like brothers. If there was any chance Montana could pull through, I don't think Smoot would have left him behind to be dog meat for a hungry posse. He figured he'd be dead before we got here."

I walked over to the soot-blackened fireplace and stared at the coals, now as dead as Montana Smith. "What'll it be, Angus?" I asked without looking back. "They got a good lead on us. Do we ride now or do we wait for first light?"

"Th' men are tired," Angus said. He spoke slowly, and in his weariness the burr in his voice was more pronounced. "Th' horses need to be grazed and rested. But I'll leave it to you, Ben. You got th' most stake in this. It's your decision."

My eyes were still on the fireplace. Suddenly it appeared like the black open mouth of a coal mine. Like the one beside the Clinch Mountains in Virginia that crippled Pa and turned him to drink.

I wanted to ride *now*! I wanted to be after Smoot and Bayliss and the tinhorn gambler. They killed Abby! They stole the life from her body! They snuffed out that special light in her eyes and stilled the pleasing lilt of her voice. Her warmth and gentleness and goodness were now only a memory.

Every fiber of my being ached with the desire to have them in my gun sight. I wanted to kill each one of them the way I had killed Montana Smith. Only quicker!

Still, I knew the odds were against us. Darkness covered their tracks. Even with a fresh start in the morning, we might never catch up to them. They'd be drinking beer and pinching dance hall girls in Fort Worth and laughing at the posse stumbling blinding through the wilderness.

At first, deep in thought, I didn't hear the gentle tapping on the roof. Then it became a roar, like a herd of longhorns stampeding over our heads.

Thunder cracked in the distance. Water gushed off the roof in torrents. Still more rain found cracks in the roof and began to puddle on the dirt floor of the shack.

"I guess that's your answer, Angus," I said, my voice heavy with emotion.

"Aye," he said sadly. "And for tomorrow, too. There won't be a track left after this gullywasher. We'll never find them."

Barely above a whisper, I said. "Maybe not tonight, Angus. Maybe not tomorrow. But soon."

Chapter Thirteen

We buried Abby on a cool and sunless spring day beside her flower garden. The clouds were dark and threatening. A distant rumbling sounded from the north. It seemed that God was angry at the needless death of someone so young and beautiful and gentle and full of life.

The mourners overflowed the tiny Presbyterian church. We had made many friends during the short time we had been in San Miguel, and Abby had won the heart of every person she had met.

"God has seen fit to take Abby from our bosom," said Angus in his eulogy.

"But the years we have known her were like a gift from heaven. She was our sunshine. She was our inspiration. She radiated joy and happiness and peace. God has made her an angel in heaven, but she was an angel on earth, too. She was a bonny lass, and I loved her like a daughter."

Angus stopped, his voice overcome with emotion. Then he said, "May God rest her soul and give her peace. And may he give peace to those who loved her."

Angus meant that last for me.

I had said little since we had ridden back with the body of Montana Smith lashed to a saddle. But my brooding silence told Angus that I was not about to give up my vow to seek out Abby's killers.

Most of the mourners from the church followed the wagon bearing the coffin out to our small ranch. They gathered around the grave, dug the day before, and sang "Rock of Ages" and "Nearer My God to Thee" to the accompaniment of a squeeze box.

Over her grave, Angus recited, *"Thou'll break my heart, thou warbling bird, That wantons thro' the flowering thorn! Thou minds me o' departed joys, Departed never to return."*

Afterward I listened to the condolences of our friends. I'm not very good at that sort of thing, but they accepted my stoicism as a sign of my grief. Which, in fact, it was.

I was filled with grief beyond words. Abby had brought me a peace and contentment I had never known before. I had been headstrong, reckless, and frequently wild before I met her in that Yankee prison camp. She had gentled me, and now I feared that wildness was about to be unleashed again. I had every intention of bringing her killers to justice. My fear was that my passion for vengeance would consume me.

The ladies had laid out a repast for the mourners. I had no taste for food.

Chago Duran approached me. He was wearing tight black clothes, and his sombrero hung down over his back. He had a red sash across his waist. His bronzed, handsome face was somber.

"Amigo," he said softly, *"La señora was una graciosa dama. Mi compasion.* I know what is in your heart. Remember, my right hand is ready to serve you and my *pistola* is yours."

"You are a true friend, *amigo*," I said, putting my hand on his shoulder. "I appreciate the offer, and, who knows, I may take you up on it. But it's going to be a long, hard trail. I couldn't ask you, or any man, to do that."

"Where you ride, I would ride. You remember that."

"I will," I said gratefully.

Only a few people were left. The ladies cleaned dishes and put away the food.

"You haven't touched a thing," said Maude Stanley, the storekeeper's wife. She was a pleasant-faced woman with a stout body that had given birth to seven children. She had a covered dish in her hands.

"I couldn't eat, Maude. Not now."

"Well, a body's gotta have nourishment," she said. "I'm gonna put a few things in the house for you. Plenty of chicken left. I got a nice potato casserole here. And there's a good slab of vinegar pie left. Made it myself. Some fresh-baked bread. I'll set them on the kitchen table. Now, you eat, hear?"

"Yes, ma'am," I promised.

Dusty had his hat in his hand and looked more awkward than I had ever seen him. His long blond hair was parted in the middle and darkened by a liberal dose of oil to keep his unruly locks in place. He wore a black suit, but it looked like an ill-fitting hand-me-down that emphasized his slight frame. His head barely reached to my shoulders. He looked scrawny, but I suspected he was as tough as rawhide.

"Mr. Wheeler," he stammered, his eyes on the ground, "I gotta tell you, but—it's just tearin' me up somethin' fierce, Mr. Wheeler."

"Just let it come out, Dusty. Don't hold it back."

"I—I don't know how to say it. I'm afraid you're gonna get mad." He glanced up at me with reddened eyes, then stared at the ground again. He twisted his hat in his hands.

"I—I loved her, Mr. Wheeler!" he blurted as he wiped at his eyes. "I mean, gosh, she's your wife—but I—I just loved her and I miss her somethin' fierce!"

I put my arm around the youth's shoulders. "I know you loved her, Dusty. And I know she loved you. She told me so herself."

He looked up at me, and his hazel eyes suddenly brightened. "She did? Gosh! I mean, you're not mad at me?"

"Of course not. Abby had a big heart, and it was filled with love. It would please Abby to hear you say that."

Dusty took a deep breath and his chest puffed up. "I feel better already. I had to get it off my chest. I was scared you— She really loved me?" He wiped the last tear from his cheek with the back of a hand. "I'm still gonna miss her somethin' fierce, Mr. Wheeler. I always will."

I said softly, "So will I, Dusty. So will I."

Angus stood by the fireplace as I entered the house. I had seen the last mourner off. It was an experience that left me more exhausted than a day on roundup pulling steers out of mud holes. I dropped on the mohair couch and stretched my feet out.

Reaching for a bottle and two glasses he had put on the side table, Angus said, "The good church ladies are gone, so let's have a man's drink."

He poured two fingers into each glass, examined them, then poured another finger. He handed me one glass and stood looking down at me. The angle made Angus look taller than he was.

I took a long swallow. I was still on the couch. Angus didn't say a word. Finally I said, "Looks like you got the floor, Angus."

"Ben, I know what you're fixin' to do. I can't say that I blame you. I want them mad dogs brought to justice as much as you do."

"There's only one way to take care of a mad dog," I said.

"That's exactly what I'm talking about, Ben. You've got to let th' law take care of this."

"What law is that? The law that let them ride into town, kill Abby, and Swensen, too, and ride out again? That the law you talking about, Angus?"

"That's funny talk coming from a man who wore a badge."

"I upheld the law to the best of my ability," I said, rising from the couch to pace the length of the room. "But I also knew the limitations of the law. Sure, I sometimes stretched my authority and operated in places where my badge was just a piece of tin. But I don't think the sheriff here's gonna chase Smoot all the way to Fort Worth. I don't think the Texas Rangers're gonna follow 'em into the Nations. The federal marshal ain't gonna track 'em to Kansas. I can, and I will!"

Angus took another swallow of whisky and said, "Ben, the good book says, 'Vengeance is mine, saith the Lord.' It doesn't profit a man to take the law into his own hands."

I looked at my friend for a long time before speaking. "I remember it also says, 'An eye for an eye, and a tooth for a tooth.'"

I poured myself another drink from the bottle. "Angus, I can't turn my back on it. I can't put Abby in the ground and forget about it. I put Moses Thatcher in the ground and turned my back on it."

Angus sighed. "Ben, that was war. You shouldn't let it gnaw on you."

"War or not, that was no way to treat a man. They let him die without lifting a finger. Abby preached forgiveness, and I tried to forgive. But not this time. There's no way I can forgive . . . or forget."

"Ben, you got a future here in San Miguel," Angus pleaded. "Come next election I was thinking of proposing you for the legislature. Who knows where that could lead? Maybe the governor's mansion. You gonna throw all that away?"

"If I have to," I said, shrugging.

"What about Abby?" he said. "Remember when she said the time had come to stop living by the gun?"

"I was hoping you wouldn't bring that up, Angus. I know I made a promise to Abby. And it grieves me that I have to break it. It hurts me, believe me it does. But I can't rest until I've done what I have to do. The fire is in me, Angus. It's burning my insides, and there's only one way to quench the flames."

Angus sighed heavily. "You're a determined man, Ben Wheeler." He poured us another drink. "And a stubborn one. You remind me of myself. I know the fire that's in you. I felt it once myself, and I took up the sword. I—"

He stopped, as though he had revealed too much. He took a quick swallow and brushed an age-dappled hand against his long mustache.

Angus said, "I see that you won't be stopped." He raised his glass to me. "The least I can do is wish you well. May God look after fools."

I laughed and raised my glass to his.

Chapter Fourteen

I spent the next few days getting my affairs in order and closing out my law office.

I had a pretty good idea where to find Smoot and his gang, and I hoped it would take only a few months. Nevertheless, I had to be prepared for a longer stay if necessary. Or for the unlikely event that I might never return.

I was in my office when I heard pounding on the stairs and Otis Rankin burst through the door.

"Ben, a Ranger just rode into town!" he said breathlessly. "Come to see about the bank robbery."

I dropped the papers in my hands and asked, "Is he downstairs now?"

"No, he ain't got here yet. Somebody said he's over at the Bluebonnet washing the trail dust outa his throat."

"First things first," I said, grabbing my hat and coat. I followed Otis down the stairs into the bank.

Asa Stanley's oldest boy had been pressed into temporary duty as teller until Otis could find a permanent replacement. Jeremiah's years of apprenticeship under his father had given him an aptitude for handling money. He was in the teller's cage taking care of a customer as I walked through the bank to the front door. Jeremiah had a thatch of yellow hair that looked like a hayrick. I wondered how long before he'd be as bald as Asa.

"I'll go talk to him at the saloon," I said. I was anxious to learn what he knew about the bank robbers and their whereabouts.

"Be sure'n send him over here when you finish," said Otis. "I want to talk to him proper like in my own bank."

I entered the batwing doors of the Bluebonnet and walked swiftly to the bar. Solomon Grace was drawing beer for three cowboys farther down the ornate bar. The Italian-made bar had come by ship as far as Galveston and then was hauled overland the rest of the way.

Solomon give me a brief nod, which I returned.

I turned my back to the bar and let my eyes grow accustomed to the dark, smoky interior after the brilliant sunshine outside. A group of ranchers sat at a table near the leaded windows at the front of the saloon. Most of the other tables were occupied by cardplayers.

At the rear the Ranger sat alone at a table. His back was to a corner, and he could survey the entire saloon from his chair.

"Don't see you in here often, Mr. Wheeler," Solomon said behind me. "What'll it be?"

I turned around and said, "Bottle of whiskey and two glasses."

He reached for a bottle on the shelf behind him.

I said, "You know I got better taste than that, Solomon. I'll take one of the bottles you keep under the bar."

Wordlessly he reached under the bar and brought up a new bottle. I plunked two dollars down on the bar, took the bottle and two glasses, and headed for the rear of the saloon.

Solomon called after me, "You got change coming, Mr. Wheeler." I ignored him.

The Ranger's eyes hat not left me since I entered, and he watched me closely as I approached the table.

"Mind if I join you?" I said, displaying the bottle.

"Who might you be?" he asked.

"Name's Ben Wheeler."

He continued to stare blankly. Then a light of recognition slowly crept into his eyes. "The lawyer fella," he said finally. "Have a seat. Terrible sorry 'bout your tragedy."

"That's why I'm here," I said, uncorking the bottle and pouring us each a drink. "You're Ranger—?"

"Thaddeus Moore," he said. He accepted the drink and downed it in one gulp.

"Now, that is good whiskey," he declared. "Call me Thad. My friends do. Mmmm. Now, that is *fine* whiskey." He poured himself another drink. "Don't mind if I do. Stuff the barkeep gave me was rotgut. Good fer nothin' but wettin' yer whistle."

"What do you know about the four men who robbed the bank?" I asked.

Moore eyed me silently over his glass. He was a big, rawboned man with large gnarly hands and a weather-beaten face seamed with age and hard living. His drooping mustache and the hair showing beneath his hat were snow white. His silver badge—a circle and star—was pinned on the left breast of his vest. It was nearly concealed by his dusty black coat. From the rank smell that reached across the table and assaulted my nostrils, I guessed he hadn't been near water for a week or two. Fact is, he looked like a man who didn't have much acquaintance with either water or soap.

He studied me for a moment longer and said, "Hear you used to marshal some up in Kansas. Reckon you might have run into Bill Smoot a time or two."

"A time or two," I admitted. "I was on his trail the time he robbed the bank in Colchester. Him and Montana I know. It's the Arkie named Bayliss and the tinhorn I want to know about."

"Seems like you took good care of Montana Smith," Moore said over his drink. "Wal, anyway, that bunch rode down from Kansas. Reckon things was getting too hot for 'em. The Arkie's name is Alvin Bayliss. Calls hisself Kid Bayliss. He ain't no more'n a whelp, but he's a mean 'un. He lit outa Fort Smith two, three years ago and hitched up with Smoot. Fancies hisself a shootist. I reckon he is. They got a rope waitin' fer him in Arkansas and another'n in Kansas. Lak I said, he's a mean 'un."

He gulped down another glass of whiskey. I didn't have to wonder anymore why his huge nose was reddened by broken veins.

"You got the other'n right," he said. "He's a tinhorn fer sure, and a no 'count polecat at that. Name a Jasper Rollins. Spends more time stealing at the gamin' tables than he do with a gun. But he ties up with Smoot now and agin. Most times he works the Kansas trail towns fleecin' cowpokes outa their hard-earned cash. Dodge City, mostly.

Come winter, he's on the riverboats, tryin' a separate ranchers and cotton planters from their pocketbooks.

"Been known to stop some in Nar'lins workin' on the sports. Kinda sallow-lookin' fella from all that time indoors. Word I hear is he got caught usin' a sleeve holdout in a card game up in Kansas and killed a man. Reckon he figgered to take a little vacation in Texas until things cooled off."

"Kid Bayliss and Jasper Rollins," I repeated. "I'll remember those names."

"I 'spect you will," said Moore.

"You got any idea where they are now?"

"They lit outa Texas, that's fer sure. Bunch answerin' their description crossed th' Red River six days after th' bank robbery. Reckon they back in their old haunts in Kansas by now. Mebbe Dodge. Cattle trail ends in Dodge now. Allus been a wild place, but I hear it's wilder'n ever. If I wuz a bettin' man, I'd lay my money on Dodge."

I shifted in my chair, preparing to leave. "Thanks for the information, Thad," I said. "By the way, Otis Rankin's waiting for you over in the bank."

Moore poured another glassful. "You kin tell 'im I'll be there directly. Thanky kindly for the whiskey. Man builds up a powerful thirst on th' trail."

I got up to leave.

"I might have a few questions for you," Moore said. "Where kin I find you?"

"In Kansas," I said. "I'm riding north."

I walked over to Asa Stanley's hardware store and plunked down seventeen dollars for the Colt Cavalry Model I had killed Montana Smith with. The new Peacemakers were faster, more dependable, and more accurate than the old cap-and-ball pistols I was used to.

Asa didn't want to take my money, but I insisted. Then he wanted to throw in the belt and holster, but I told him I had one that was well worn and suited me just fine.

He pointed out the new belts had loops for extra cartridges. He put the belt and the two boxes of cartridges on the counter.

This time, he insisted.

* * *

The next morning I rode over to the Lazy A and asked Angus if he would sign me on for the cattle drive. I said I'd do it for nothing, since I'd be bringing along my own small herd.

"Kinda sudden, ain't it?" Angus said. "But you know you're always welcome. For a lawyer, you're a mighty fine trail hand."

Angus shifted in his saddle, tugged at his mustache and asked, "This mean you had a change of heart about chasing them men?"

I said, "Angus, let's just say I got reason to get to Kansas. And riding with three thousand head of cattle is as good a way to get there as any."

"Aye," Angus said. After a moment, he added, "And it attracts a lot less attention to a man."

Chapter Fifteen

I rode right swing as the long drive curved between a little roundtop hill on the east and a stand of blackjack oaks on the west.

Angus had galloped miles ahead after the nooning to look for water and a campground to bed the cattle down for the night.

Chago Duran and Ed Crayler rode pointer at the head of the column of cattle. They had veered the longhorns toward the north and Red River Station, where we would cross into Indian Territory. We would make the Red River, our first difficult river ford, in about another week. The muddy, reddish Brazos was behind us.

Dust kicked up by the cattle's steel-sharp hooves blew over me in billowing clouds. I pulled my bandanna up over my face, but the fine dust seeped through and irritated my nose. Still, it wasn't as bad as some of them had it. The day before I had been at left flank, and for three days before that had taken my turn at drag. At the rear of the drive, which was strung out like a lank rope across a mile of rolling prairie, the dust had been thick enough to plow.

Ahead of me Chago dropped back, looking like a ghostly rider emerging from a fog. He rode close to me so I could hear him over the rumble of cracking hooves and ankle joints and the rattle of colliding horns.

"Amigo," he said quietly, lest he alarm the jittery cattle. "How ees it back here?"

"They been bunching up some," I said, "but I got 'em pretty well spread out now. Not as bad as keeping 'em spaced at flank."

"Bueno. They bunch up, they get too hot."

My job was to keep the long brown ribbon of beef moving toward market and to see that they kept far enough apart to stay reasonably cool. If they got too hot, it melted the fat right out of the beef.

"You leave Alamo on point?" I asked.

"Si. Good man. He learn fast."

"I guess he can use the experience. Hard to find a good pointer."

We had eleven cowboys riding herd on the cattle, forming a box around the drive. Chago and Crayler rode at the head of the cattle at point. They were Angus's most experienced and trusted cowhands. Riding between them were Boomer and Old Stag. Those two old trail-wise steers, with bells around their necks, had led every herd Angus had driven to Kansas.

Halfway back, on each side, were the two swing riders. Near the end of the herd two cowboys rode flank on either side of the cattle. Finally, at the end of the herd came three riders at drag. They kept the back corners together, prodded the slowpokes, and ate dust. It was the only place on the drive, far from the sharp ears of the trail boss, where a rider felt it safe to curse freely without fear of a fine.

The last two riders ranged the entire length of the drive. They lent a hand where it was needed and spelled a cowboy in an emergency. Angus usually had his next most trusted hands on that job, Alamo Rehnquist and Pete Claymore. He wanted them to pick up as much experience on point as they could.

The rest of us rotated among swing, flank, and drag.

I had been on a few drives before, admittedly before the war, and had ridden point. But Angus was not a man to grant privileges merely on friendship, nor did I want any. I was only along for the one drive. I wanted to pull my own weight. The last thing I wanted was to cause any hard feelings by knocking an experienced cowhand out of his rightly earned position.

Chago, still riding beside me, said good-naturedly, "Do not spoil your appetite eating dust. Ginger will have a fine supper waiting for us in an hour or two."

I looked up at the sun. It hovered over the western horizon. Time to ease up on the cattle and let them drift out and graze until we reached the campground.

"A little tequila to wash the dust down would do nicely right now," I said.

"*Si*. I can taste the fiery liquid in my throat even now. But"—he shrugged—"you know *Señor* Finlay."

I laughed. "I sure do. Old Angus practically runs a branch of the Bluebonnet back at the Lazy A. But once he's on the drive he's got his own temperance union."

Actually, Angus's strict rules weren't whims. A drunken cowboy was a menace to himself, his horse, the cattle, and his fellow hands. Gambling often led to hard feelings, and it was tough enough keeping up morale on a three-month drive that consisted mostly of backbreaking work, sore muscles, sweat, heat, dust, and little sleep.

Angus also fined any cowboy he heard swearing, but with Angus usually ranging far ahead of the herd, that was a much-abused rule. There was hardly anybody on the drive who didn't air his lungs once in a while. The older hands believed swearing took the strain off the liver. The younger ones cursed to prove their manhood. And there was just something about a stubborn steer that provoked a man to let fly a blue streak.

Besides, every cowboy knew that when we reached market he could let off steam to his heart's content.

"Time to let the cattle graze," Chago said as he galloped off to return to point.

I swung into the line of the herd, gently waving my hat in my hand to separate the cows. My horse walked slowly beside them, and I kept my movements slow to avoid spooking the cattle. Behind me, at flank, I could see Amos Thurman working the cattle out so they could munch at the long green grass as they walked slowly along.

The three weeks since we had left the Lazy A had been relatively peaceful. We had not had a serious stampede. Our toughest time came in the first two weeks, before the cattle were road broke.

We had to constantly fight the cows' natural instinct to turn back to their native feeding ground. Several times small groups at the rear of the drive had broken off and stampeded for home. It was tough, tense work keeping the other beeves from joining them. We spent many hours waving our hats and snapping our slickers to turn the ornery critters back to rejoin the herd.

Angus, acting as his own trail boss, rode at the head. Most days we didn't see him for hours at a time. He scouted far ahead, looking for water, selecting the noon stops, finding the right campgrounds with sweet water and plenty of grass.

I never asked Angus why he was his own ramrod. But I suspected it was partly out of his own parsimonious nature and partly because he enjoyed it so much.

A trail boss was like a general moving an army across the land. It required courage, resourcefulness, strength, brains, and a hell of a lot of experience. All of which Angus had to spare. The secret of success lay in finding grass and water, with water being the most important. Nobody was better at it than Angus.

The cook wagon, carrying Ginger and Horse, also stayed far ahead of the drive. They stopped twice a day, for the noon meal and for supper.

The wagon, pulled by a brace of mules Ginger had named Sorry and Sinful, had been copied from the original made by Angus's old friend, Charlie Goodnight. Our blanket rolls, rifles, slickers, axle grease, and sacks of flour, sugar, salt, beans, onions, potatoes, and whatnot went on the wagon protected by the canvas cover. On the side hung a huge water barrel and on the other a toolbox. Slung beneath the wagon was a rawhide cooney to hold the firewood.

But the most important part, at the rear, was the chuck box.

The chuck box had a dozen drawers and cubbyholes that were revealed when the lid was swung down to form a worktable. Secreted in those drawers and cubbyholes was a wonderland of everything Ginger needed to fill our stomachs, patch our wounds, or sew on a loose button.

Ginger could also satisfy a cowboy's craving for a chaw of tobaccy or the fillings of a quirley to go with a cup of coffee strong enough to melt a shootin' iron.

Rattling in the boot beneath the chuck box were an assortment of skillets, Dutch ovens, and the paraphernalia of cookery.

The chuck wagon also carried the trail drive's only bottle of whiskey. Or, at least, the only known bottle. It was strictly for medicinal purposes. I've heard it said that after a month of enforced abstinence on the trail some cowboys have been known to offer a bare leg to a sidewinder.

Caesar trotted along beside the wagon, sometimes veering off to chase a rabbit. Occasionally he hopped onto the wagon to sit beside Ginger, or he settled in the back for a snooze. Angus tolerated the presence of a dog, which could easily spook the cattle, only on Ginger's solemn oath that Caesar would behave himself.

Behind the chuck wagon, and off to one side, came Zack Freeman driving a remuda of sixty horses. Most of them were stocky mustang ponies with plenty of cow sense. Zack kept them far enough ahead so that the spirited animals wouldn't frighten the herd, yet close enough so that a fresh mount was readily available when needed.

The isolation seemed to suit the former slave turned wrangler just fine. It kept him away from the taunts of the cowboys, who took to bigotry as easily as they took to horses. The men respected Zack's ability with a horse. No one questioned that he was the best breaker on the ranch. Still, no one wanted to sit down and eat with him.

The tall, bony, swaybacked longhorns moved slowly. They stopped frequently to chew at the grass. I prodded them now and again to keep them moving, and I watched that they didn't drift too far from the line of the drive. Their big heads dipped often to bite off the tall grass. Their horns flashed in the sun. Every now and then one cracked against another, producing a sharp report. They were used to the sound and were rarely startled by it.

Occasionally, too, a lumbering beast raised its head like a suspicious sentinel. Her eyes grew wilder and her nostrils flared as she sought the smell of water. I watched closely for any sign of trouble, but after a moment the cow would dip her head for another mouthful of grass.

We left the blackjacks behind and moved onto an expanse of rolling prairie. The green grass was dotted with patches of bluebonnets and yellow blossoms of wild mustard. Stunted mesquite trees thrust out young, lacy foliage.

I could feel the restlessness of the cattle as they grew eager for water.

It would be dark in another hour or two. We had to get the cattle watered and bedded down before we lost the light.

Far ahead, on the highest ground, Angus turned his horse broadside to us. He raised his hat and circled it over his head. Each rider passed on the signal to camp until it reached the men at drag. It was a welcome sign to the weary, hungry cowboys.

The cattle, smelling water, rushed eagerly for the creek at the bottom of a rise. The cowhands worked together to keep the cattle from pushing and crowding as each drank its fill.

We moved the cattle just beyond the creek and rode them into a compact herd off the trail. There was plenty of grass, and they ate with a strong appetite.

Chapter Sixteen

Chago and Crayler ate first, as was their due as pointers.

Neither spoke to the other except when absolutely necessary. Each took his plate and sat far from the other. Crayler to show his contempt for Chago's exotic foreignness, and Chago to show his contempt for Crayler's bigotry and cowardice.

Zack set up the remuda by the chuck wagon. Dusty, being the greenest of the greenhorns, held the end of a rope stretched from a wagon wheel as one boundary. The horses were used to the routine, although a few bent on wandering were hobbled by Zack. Once they were assembled, Dusty lowered the rope.

I was unsaddling my horse and putting him in the remuda when I heard Crayler's loud voice from the other side of the wagon.

"Now you take settin' up a remuda, that's nigger work," Crayler said.

As I came around the wagon, I saw Chago eyeing Crayler with hatred. Crayler avoided any direct confrontation with Chago. He feared the proud young Mexican, although he called him a "greaser" behind his back. Chago kept his distance and temper out of loyalty to Angus.

Zack and Dusty had their plates out for Ginger to fill.

Crayler, sitting by his empty plate, called, "Hey, Ginger! Got any chitlins for them two darkies?" He laughed at his own crude jest. "Mebbe a mess a greens, too! Them niggers taken to rabbit food."

Zack, long used to absorbing punishment, said nothing.

Dusty said, "You got a big mouth, Mr. Crayler!"

"Mebbe you'd like to do somethin' about it, sonny boy," Crayler taunted.

When he got no answer, he added, "Naw, I thought not. You still wet behind th' ears, boy. Yore mama know where you at?"

Chago casually took out his gun, checked to see that it was fully loaded, spun the cylinder, and dropped it back into his holster. The gesture was not lost on Crayler. His squint eye almost closed, he anxiously sought a new diversion. The ugly red scar on his cheek was still a reminder of his behavior at the line shack.

Caesar came loping along and stopped in front of Crayler. He sniffed at his plate for any leftovers. Crayler drew back an arm menacingly.

"Git away from me, ya lousy mutt!" he snarled. "Damned dog ain't got no business on a cattle drive nohow."

Very slowly Ginger picked up his meat cleaver and took a step toward Crayler.

Angus stepped into the firelight from nowhere and said, "Ed, you know my rules about cussin'. That's twenty-five cents comin' outa your wages when we get to Kansas."

Ginger set down the cleaver and spooned food into Zack's plate.

"Twenty-five cents?" Crayler protested. "I only said one word, Mr. Finlay."

"Two words. In my book, nigger's a cuss word, too."

Crayler remained silent. He lowered his eyes, and as he shuffled off, he murmured, "Jes' funnin'. Dint mean no harm."

By the time I grabbed a tin plate and some eating irons, Tom Kelly and Pete Claymore were scraping their plates. Tom and Pete had first night watch. In a few minutes they'd saddle their night mounts and take up their stations riding slowly around the herd in opposite directions. Soon we'd hear their soft crooning to the cattle.

Ford Burkhardt, a bowlegged bantamweight only a couple of years older than Dusty, stood in front of me holding out his plate. "I'm so hungry I could eat a saddle," he said. "Whatcha got tonight, Ginger?"

"You want a menu, go to a restaurant," Ginger said sourly. He dumped stew and beans into Burkhardt's plate.

"Pecos strawberries again?" Burkhardt said in mock disappointment. Despite the derisive term, the cowboys ravenously ate the beans Ginger had cooked over a slow fire and seasoned with dry salt pork.

I silently held out my plate for Ginger to fill. I grabbed a handful of sourdough biscuits he had baked in a Dutch oven and spooned dry fruit onto my plate. I filled my tin cup with steaming black coffee and found a grassy spot to sit cross-legged and eat.

I had the ten-to-twelve watch. I doubted that I'd get much sleep until I was relieved. And very little after that, because we would rise before dawn to get the cattle watered and grazed and on the drive again.

Amos Thurman, resting his back against a wagon wheel, pulled a harmonica out of a shirt pocket. He tapped it several times against his palm and began playing the mournful strains of "Red River Valley."

Angus, a plate in one hand and a cup in the other, sat down beside me.

"Crayler's the most experienced hand I got," Angus said wearily. "He's got almost as much cow sense as a cuttin' horse. But he's sure pushin' me to the edge. Man was raised on sour milk. I got half a mind to pay him off at Red River Station."

I shoveled a handful of raisins into my mouth, then took a bite of dried apple. As I chewed, I asked, "Getting pretty close to the Nations. What you figure, another week?"

Angus nodded. "Six, seven days, if we don't have a stampede. And if the weather holds."

I said, "Four weeks to cross the Nations. Another two, three weeks to get to Dodge. They moved the Spanish tick quarantine again. Dodge is as good a place as any to start looking. Don't matter. I'll find 'em."

"Kinda hopin' hard work'd sweat that notion outa ya."

"Ain't much else to think about, Angus. They killed Abby, and they're going to answer for it. That's the size of it."

Angus took a long swig of coffee. "You're a stubborn man, Ben." He was silent for several minutes as he ate. Finally he said, "I admire a stubborn man. One myself." He wolfed the rest of his food down and got to his feet. "I got work to do. Ain't much rest on a cattle drive."

I dug my blanket roll out of the wagon. Horse cleaned the tin plates and utensils we had dumped into the wrecking pan. Ginger studied the sky for a while. Then he picked up the wagon tongue and pointed it toward the North Star. In the morning it would show us due north.

Several cowboys puffed on hand-rolled quirleys. The smell of the burning tobacco mingled with that of the fire and supper.

I spread my blanket roll, hoping I could get a few winks before watch. Amos played "Goodbye, Old Paint," then launched into "Green Grow the Lilacs."

That's the last thing I remembered until I heard someone softly calling my name. I stirred and heard my name again. It was time for my night watch. A cowboy always woke his relief by calling his name. He never touched a sleeping cowboy, lest he come up with a gun in his hand.

I'd slept in my clothes, so I was ready to go after a wake-up cup of some of Ginger's awesome coffee.

I found my night mount in the bright moonlight. I patted her and spoke a few soothing words into her ear as I threw on a blanket and saddle. I pulled the latigo tight and mounted.

Bill Daffern and I had the ten-to-midnight watch. I rode clockwise and he rode counterclockwise. Bill had a fine Irish tenor voice, and he softly crooned "The Old Chisholm Trail."

Come me along, boys, and listen to my tale:
I'll tell you of my troubles on the Old Chisholm Trail.
Come a ti yi yippy, yippy yay, yippy yay,
Come a ti yi yippy, yippy yay.

Now, I couldn't carry a tune in a bucket. Still, I did the best I could with "The Horse Wrangler" and "Bury Me Not on the Lone Prairie." The cows never complained, but when my voice got too flat I switched to humming. The cattle found it reassuring, so that was all that mattered.

Most of the herd was lying down, chewing cuds, and blowing. A few still munched on grass.

I kept one eye on the herd and the other on the lookout for marauders. Under the nearly full moon I could see the herd clearly and watched for any sign of a stampede.

Bill and I passed twice each round. Each time we exchanged a few words.

"Quiet night."

"Yup. Any sign of coyotes?"

"Heard 'em in the hills, 's all."

The longhorns, encouraged by the bright moon, began to rise and browse. Some only changed positions and sank immediately to their knees and resettled themselves. The cattle yawned and browsed. I yawned, too. I pulled out a piece of dried apple I had tucked into a pocket. It gave me something to graze on.

I studied the night sky. The Big Dipper was due west of the North Star and hanging down. The next time I passed Bill, I said, "Time to hit the sack."

Bill nodded, and I rode off to wake our relief.

I didn't need a lullaby. I was asleep the instant my head hit the blanket roll.

Chapter Seventeen

"Grub *pi-i-i-l-le!*"

My eyes snapped open. It was still dark, but the sun, below the horizon, had turned the eastern sky a bright pink. I sat up and pulled my boots on.

"Git up, you lazy critters!" Ginger barked. "Get up and greet the day, or I'm gonna dump this mess a grub for the coyotes to fight over."

The men around me stirred and sat up. I strapped on my gunbelt, set my hat on my head, and rolled up my bedroll. With the smell of frying bacon and coffee filling my senses, I walked down to the creek to splash cold water on my face.

The call of a meadowlark came from a thicket near the water.

I poured myself a cup of coffee, yawned, and took a sip of the scalding liquid.

Ginger pulled sourdough out of his keg by the handful. He slapped it onto a board, worked in salt and lard, dropped in raisins, and kneaded the dough. He cut the biscuits with a tin cup. He placed the biscuits in a Dutch oven set on the glowing coals and heaped more coals on the lid.

"Horace!" he growled. "Stop standin' round like an idjit and grab a bucket and get me some water from th' crick!"

Horse jumped and took off for the creek as though a pack of howling wolves was snapping at his heels.

Angus, always the first man up, had already eaten and was on horseback supervising the last night watch in getting the cattle watered.

Caesar watched from his perch on the seat of the chuck wagon as Ginger served Crayler and Chago first. Crayler eyed the hound as he took a fistful of biscuits and poured molasses into his plate. The dog bared his teeth.

"Hey, Ginger, you gonna make some red bean pie tonight?" Burkhardt asked eagerly. "Man, my mouth's sure waterin' for some a yore red bean pie."

Ginger eyes him scornfully. "I was thinkin' on it," he said, "but you just changed my mind."

Burkhardt's face dropped.

Ginger opened a can of Arbuckle's coffee and took out the peppermint stick packed inside and put it in an apron pocket.

Burkhardt mumbled under his breath, "Prolly gonna save the candy fer his dawg."

Ginger looked up sharply. "You say somethin', cowboy?"

"Uh, I said them biscuits look dawg-gone good."

Ginger was an object of great speculation among the cowboys. We knew his name was George Pittman, and that was about it. We also knew he was the best damn ranch cook, bar none. His son-of-a-bitch stew was second to none. His red bean pie was known to have lured a top cowhand from another ranch. He knew his beans and onions, but whatever else he knew, he kept to himself.

He kept the men's stomachs satisfied, but he was not a man to be trifled with. He was as handy with a gun as he was with a meat cleaver, and he was apt to grab up either one if a man gave him offense. Every man steered clear of offending Ginger, although Crayler's grudge against Caesar was as close as any man ever got.

There was general agreement among the cowboys that if ever a man killed Ginger he would be lynched on the spot.

No man knew where Ginger came from, and no one dared ask. I doubt that any man had ever seen Ginger without a shirt or his long underwear. They were as ever-present as his derby and red suspenders. Still a few men swore they had seen sailor's tattoos on his arms. Ginger did roll a bit when he walked, but that was a gait peculiar to both sailors and cowboys.

No one questioned Ginger about his origin, the sea, or anything else. Not only was it range etiquette never to inquire about a man's background, but in Ginger's case it could lead to punishment a man could feel in his taste buds and growling stomach.

Once, on a roundup, the rumor started that Ginger had killed a man and that's why he left the sea. If that rumor ever reached Ginger's ears, he never acknowledged it.

The only cowboy on the drive Ginger seemed to tolerate was Dusty. The way he showed it was by not snarling at Dusty as much as he did at the rest of us. He also occasionally rewarded Dusty with the peppermint stick that came in the can of Arbuckle's coffee.

The only affection he ever displayed was toward Caesar, a dog as surly and as unpleasant as his master. Every man gave Caesar a wide berth, except Dusty. Caesar was sometimes seen trotting along after Dusty, his tail wagging. That didn't escape the notice of Ginger. Which might explain his tolerance of the green young cowhand.

I chewed bacon and sopped the light, fluffy raisin biscuits in molasses. The other men around me ate with silent dedication.

Bill Daffern stifled a yawn and took a big swig of strong black coffee in the hope it would wake him up.

"Man," Bill said, "I ain't missed this much sleep since that time we delivered a herd to Newton. I swear I dint go to bed for a week. Wal," he said, grinning, "I did go to bed, but not to sleep."

"That the time you almost had to marry that prairie dove?" Amos asked, taking a tobacco sack from his shirt pocket and rolling a quirley.

"Naw, that was in Abilene three years ago."

"I remember that," said Alamo. "She went to Wild Bill Hickok hisself and swore you'd promised to marry her."

"Was that Wild Bill?" Daffern asked. "I don't recollect. My memory's a little fuzzy."

Alamo guffawed loudly. "Wal, mine ain't. You pert near killed your pony lightin' a shuck for Texas."

Burkhardt said, "Hey, Ben. You was marshal up in Kansas fer a spell. How'd you handle this Irish lover?"

"Jail, I reckon." I paused. "For his own protection."

"Yeah," said Alamo. "Some a them calico queens carry Arkansas toothpicks."

"Take yore gizzard right out," added Burkhardt.

"Laugh, you mangy lot," Daffern said, "but when we get to Dodge I'll drink any man under the table. *And* I'll have a cowboy queen on each arm!"

"Double reason to get you in trouble," said Alamo.

The talk around the camp fire frequently returned to the end of the trail. No matter in what direction the conversation began, thoughts of bellying up to the bar with a fistful of dollars always intruded.

Somebody could complain about the lack of sleep, for instance. And Bill Daffern was likely to say, "You'll stay 'wake longer'n this once we get to Dodge, and you'll call it fun."

"You been there?" asked Thurman.

"Once. Two, three years ago. Queen of the Cowtowns, they call it. Used ta call it Buffalo City. Got more painted cats than Abilene ever thought about. They got nineteen saloons in Dodge. Mueller's, the Alhambra, Long Branch, Alamo. Place growin' so fast they still got tents."

"Every cowtown's got an Alamo Saloon," said Thurman.

"Yeah," said Daffern. "Wait'll you see Chalkley Beeson's Saratoga. Old Chalk's got hisself an orchestra. You can dance till your boots fall off."

Pete Claymore said. "I think my boots 'bout ready to fall off right now."

Crayler, who had been eyeing Daffern with a surly expression, said, "Daffern, you worsen a damn Mex thinkin' on pleasures."

Daffern laughed. "Trouble with you, Ed, is you think on th' hardships. Turn a man's milk sour. I think on them pleasure palaces on the Arkansas just waitin' for this old boy from Texas."

Crayler sneered. "Wal, you figger on reachin' them pleasure palaces, you stay outa my way."

Daffern did not change his amiable expression. His voice stayed even. "I guess my ears playin' tricks on me," he said. "Them sounded like threatenin' words. And here I ain't no Mex or nigger or no green-horn."

Crayler dropped the bridle he was holding and stood facing Daffern with one hand on the butt of his gun. "You sayin' I'm yella?"

Daffern, still smiling, replied, "I'm sayin' anytime you feel like takin' on a *real* man, I'll be here."

Crayler stared at Daffern, a thin rail of a man with a shock of light brown hair, rosy cheeks, and laugh lines around his eyes. He was a man just barely into his twenties. He returned his gaze until Crayler slowly picked up the bridle and walked off.

Crayler never seemed to benefit from any of his experiences. Even after he was shamed, he was back at it again. Picking at it, picking at it, like a man with a sore that wouldn't stop itching.

His frequent target was Dusty, and it took very little to set him off.

"I want to learn to handle a forty-four like a real shootist," Dusty said one day at breakfast. "You reckon you can learn me?"

There was a loud guffaw from behind me. Crayler, clad only in dingy woolen underwear, was shaving himself at a mirror propped on a wheel of the chuck wagon. He worked the razor carefully around the scar on his cheek.

Crayler, lather still on his face, said, "A shootist? Mebbe you kin hit a tin can on a fence post, sonny boy, but a tin can don't shoot back. Somebody shoot back, you'd pee in yore pants."

Dusty furiously charged at Crayler. "That's a dastardly lie! You take that back."

"Fack's a fack," said Crayler, wiping his razor.

"Ain't neither no fack!" Dusty fumed.

Dusty swung from the ground. His fist connected squarely with Crayler's jaw. The big man dropped his razor and staggered back against the wagon wheel. He shook his head, then rushed the wiry little cowboy. He wrapped his bearlike arms around Dusty and squeezed the breath out of him.

I was on my feet and running toward them, but Ginger got there first. He had the meat cleaver in his hand and fire in his eyes. Caesar, crouching low, bared his fangs and growled menacingly.

"Ed Crayler!" Ginger said between clenched teeth. "Turn that boy loose or I'm gonna split your head open like a watermelon!"

Crayler looked at the cook. Ginger raised the cleaver over his head. Crayler quickly released Dusty.

"One day, sonny boy," Crayler hissed, "you ain't gonna have 'Daddy' round to save yore hide."

Ginger said, "One day I ain't gonna say howdy. I'm just gonna lay this cleaver betwix yore ears."

Crayler moved back a step. In a parting sally, he said, "Time for yore lollipop, sonny boy!"

He spun on his heels and left.

Chapter Eighteen

We camped for two days near Red River Station, waiting for the herds ahead of us to cross.

Ginger spent the time at Doan's general store, restocking the chuck wagon. He traded newborn calves to some of the Montague County farmers for onions and potatoes. He also got a fresh supply of greens, although everybody except Angus, Zack, and myself spurned it as "rabbit food."

The rest of us spent what little time Angus allowed us away from the herd at the tiny settlement's one saloon, getting reacquainted with John Barleycorn. It was our last chance to blow off steam before the hazardous trek across the Indian Territory into Kansas.

Angus scouted the river all the way to the mouth of Fleetwood Branch and back, and watched as the other herds forded the river.

"I've crossed the Red many a time," he said. "I know the best place from the year before. I know where the quicksand pits were the last time. But you can't trust last year when it comes to a river. It's a living thing, changing constantly."

So, for two days Angus stood on the banks and watched the cowboys swim herds across to the Indian Territory. He didn't mind the wait.

Besides the chance to study the river, it gave him another opportunity to fatten the herd and rest his weary crew.

"It'll take a month to cross the Indian Territory," he announced at breakfast the day before we were to ford the river.

"That's about as fast as you can push the cattle and men. And I'm going to push very hard. We got a lot of rivers to cross. God willing, none are in the flood stage. We got a lot of dangerous prairie to cross. Word is the Kiowas and Comanches are on the move. I hear a couple of herds got hit within the week. One lost two hundred head of beef. The other about half that."

Angus sopped a biscuit in molasses and popped it into his mouth. "By the Almighty, I don't intend to lose any steers to heathens!"

I lighted a cigar and sat back to enjoy the smoke with my coffee. I'd bought a fresh supply at Doan's. "Suppose," I said, "you have to part with a few head to buy peace with the hostiles?"

Angus looked at me with his hard blue eyes. Like flint, sparks seemed to fly from them. Finally he said, "Aye, but there's a difference between what I choose to donate for a worthy cause and what a man wants to take from me at gunpoint."

I sucked deep on my cigar, then blew out the white smoke. "That being the case, I could point out a few troublemakers I've spotted on the trail."

Angus laughed and said, "Nae, you won't be rid of them that easy. Troublemakers or not, they still bring a bonny price in Kansas."

The local Texas Ranger was named Tom Worthy, and he had one of those keep-your-distance looks. He wasn't an easy man to talk to. He was barrel-chested and bandy-legged, and although just into his thirties, he'd already lost most of his hair. His eyes almost disappeared as he squinted at me in the tiny one-room shack that was both his office and living quarters.

"You got some kind a warrant fer these desperadoes?" he asked suspiciously.

"No, I'm afraid not," I said.

"Mebbe you oughta stop in to see the federal judge in Fort Smith. But I don't reckon he kin help you if you ain't some kind a lawman."

"I carried a badge once," I said.

"Don't cut it now," he said. "Don't take kindly, either, to vigilantes or bounty hunters."

I was starting to lose my temper, but I tried to keep it in check. I didn't want to be clapped into jail by some overzealous protector of law and order.

I said, "I talked to Ranger Moore, and he told me the three of them crossed the Red—"

"I used to ride with Thad," Worthy said. "He's a mite windy."

"—River and headed for Kansas."

"That's about what I heard, too," he admitted.

"What else you heard?"

Worthy studied me for a moment before answering.

"They killed yore wife?"

I nodded.

"Most likely the Kid," he said. "I tangled with him once near Texarkana. Shoulda kilt him when I had the chance."

"The Kid pulled the trigger," I said, "but the rest were in on it."

"I reckon so. Only thing I heared was Smoot's a mite active again in Kansas and Missouri. Robbed a train. You ridin' north with a herd, mos' likely you'll find him in Kansas."

"Kansas is a big state."

Worthy smiled for the first time. "Yeah, but Smoot makes a lotta noise."

That night we whooped it up for the last time in the saloon. We were due to cross at daybreak.

We left two men on guard to see that our herd didn't mingle with the herds coming up behind us to wait their turn at the river.

Ginger, as always, stayed in camp, but he had a jug. He was a solitary drinker. He shunned the companionship of sharing drinks and swapping stories. On such nights, Horse, who had never tasted liquor in his twenty-seven years, sat by silently. When Ginger fell into a stupor, Horse tucked him into his blanket roll. Afterward Horse crawled into the cooney and fell fast asleep.

Zack Freeman also stayed behind. He had to look after the horses. But, more importantly, he would not be welcomed in the saloon. In fact, the black man would be risking his life if he walked through the doors. Zack wasn't much of a drinking man, but Angus saw that he had a bottle

92

of the sour mash bourbon he favored. It was one of the few times Angus allowed whiskey in camp.

Daffern surveyed the close interior of the saloon and said above the din, "It ain't much of a saloon, but I reckon it'll have to do until we get to Dodge."

He was right. It wasn't much of a saloon. It was a slapped-together affair of adobe brick and green pine boards. It had a dirt floor, and the bar was nothing but planks laid across whiskey barrels. Not only was it noisy, but its smoky interior was hot and airless.

The quality of its whiskey was no better.

"I've seen worse," said Alamo.

"And I've seen better," said Daffern.

I was standing beside Dusty, who was nursing a lukewarm beer, when Crayler elbowed his way to the bar.

"Barkeep," he said, "I want whiskey." He looked at Dusty. "And my little friend here will have sarsaparilla—iffen you serve chil'run in this here man's bar."

Dusty started to protest, but Crayler cut him short.

Thumping the youth hard on the chest, he said, "I doan take sass from you, sonny boy. You doan pull yore weight on the drive, an' you ain't got none to throw round here. Yore big daddy ain't here with his meat cleaver."

Dusty started to protest again. This time I stopped him.

Facing Crayler, I said, "I'm getting awfully tired of you. I don't like the way you bully people you think can't fight back."

Along the bar the drinkers started moving back. Those who had not heard my soft-spoken words were warned by others. Crayler and I had the bar to ourselves. Even the barkeep moved back to a safe distance.

I said, "Crayler, I'm going to tell you this one time, so you damn well better remember it. I don't take kindly to your kind. You push Dusty around—or anyone else—and I'm going to take it real personal. You won't get off as easy as the last time you crossed me."

I kept my right hand free, ready to go for my gun. But I doubted there'd be any need for it. When Crayler looked at me briefly, his squint eye almost closed, I could see there would be no need for it. He would never draw on a man familiar with the ways of a gun.

He turned his eyes away and started to leave.

I grabbed him by his leather vest and pulled him back. My face was only inches away from his. I said, "There is nothing more contemptible than a bully. In case you don't understand me, I'm talking about you, Crayler. Now, get outa my sight! You remember what I told you—or by God you'll answer for it!"

Crayler couldn't get out of there fast enough. I didn't like shaming a man in front of the men he worked with, but Crayler set my teeth on edge. Besides, I knew Crayler wasn't a man to stay shamed. Or to remember a lesson. He would be up to his old tricks in a few days.

I was surprised when the other cowboys patted me on the back. Daffern bought me a drink. Thurman said, "That son of a bitch had it comin'!" Pete Claymore said, "Damn, it's about time somebody taken on Crayler!"

Everybody wanted to tell Crayler off, but everybody was waiting for the next man to do it.

The only unhappy cowboy was Dusty. I let him mope for a while, then steered him to a corner table.

"Doan need nobody to fight my fights," he protested, keeping his head down. "I ain't no baby."

"No, you sure ain't," I said. "You're damn near a growed man, and you do a man's job. Angus Finlay would never abide a man who didn't know his job or who slacked."

"I kin ride as good as any man."

"That's a fact," I said. "You can rope like a buckaroo, and if ever a man was born with cow sense, it was you."

He looked up and his face brightened.

"But you still got some growing up to do," I said. "And you still got a lot of learning ahead of you."

"Mr. Finlay said the drive would make a man of me."

"He's right. It will."

"Then I kin fight my own fights."

I didn't answer him directly. I said, "Dusty, I seen pride kill more men than any other reason. They got provoked into something they couldn't handle, and their pride wouldn't let 'em ease out of it. When a man gets his pride up, his common sense goes out the window."

"You sayin' I shouldn't stand up to Mr. Crayler?"

"I'm saying you shouldn't let your pride speak for you. Crayler was trying to provoke you into going for your gun. If it goes to gunplay, you wouldn't live to see the sunrise. You haven't got the experience, but it's going to come. When I was your age, I worked on a ranch down near Corpus Christi. I was just like you, full of piss and vinegar. But I wouldn't be here today if I hadn't had somebody looking out for me until I learned to take care of myself. It don't shame a boy to have somebody teaching him the ropes and looking after him."

Dusty smiled and took a gulp of beer. "That means you gonna learn me the ropes, Mr. Wheeler?"

"I couldn't ask for a better pupil," I said.

Chapter Nineteen

Old Stag was reluctant to enter the water.

He twisted his big, woolly head around obstinately. The bell tied to his neck clanked in protest.

a"Let's get this big swimmin' on!" ordered Angus, who stood to one side with the Texas cattle inspectors.

Chago swatted the stubborn steer's rump with his riata. The beast refused to budge. Behind Old Stag, Boomer and three thousand head of cattle watched with wild, apprehensive eyes. The cattle started to bunch up because the cowboys in the rear, unaware of the holdup, kept prodding the herd forward.

Crayler, his horse poised to plunge into the water with the first of the herd, spit on the ground. "Damn Mex!" he swore. "Cain't even git a critter into the water."

Alamo rode into the midst of the cattle at the river's edge and swung his hat wildly from side to side.

"Heeeee yaaaaaah!" he yelled. "Git along!" He whistled shrilly between his teeth. The first movement was detected among the reluctant cattle.

A lumbering red steer, its horns reaching nearly five feet across, shoved his way to the front and stepped boldly into the river. He sank in until all that was visible were his woolly head, bulging eyes, flaring nostrils, and those magnificent horns.

He swam strongly for the other shore.

Old Stag watched the upstart for a minute, then plunged in. There was no holding them back after that. The river filled with cattle, churning the muddy water, protesting loudly, and heading for the opposite bank.

"By golly," cried Angus, "he shamed Old Stag into it!"

As an afterthought, he bellowed, "Mark that steer! We got more rivers to cross!" From his horseback headquarters, Angus issued a series of orders as the crossing proceeded.

The inspectors, tally sheets in hand, stood in the shade of a grove of cottonwood trees and watched the crossing closely.

They examined the road brand, looking for cattle that didn't belong in the herd. They were looking for stolen cattle. But many herds picked up strays on the drive, so they were also checking to see that they had been properly branded.

Earlier a couple of gents claiming to be trail cutters had appeared and said they were going to cut out the strays. Angus took exception to that, so they offered to settle for fifty dollars each. Angus took even more exception to that. The two gents left in a hurry, lucky that they weren't horsewhipped first.

Nearby was a scattering of graves of cowboys who had died attempting to cross the river.

A tangle of brush along the riverbank was caught in the roots of trees half in the water and half out. The next flood, tearing at the riverbank, would sweep some of the trees downstream. Driftwood was caught in some of the trees higher than a man's head, testimony to past floods.

We broke camp at daybreak that day and drove the herd straightaway to the fording site Angus had selected.

We stowed our boots, gunbelts, and unnecessary clothing in the wagon, and Ginger took it across on the ferry. A few cowboys stripped down to a pair of pants, myself included, and some rode bareback to keep their saddles dry. Not only would the extra gear weigh us down, but no one wanted to get it wet.

Ginger and Horse rode on to set up camp at the site Angus had pointed out the day before.

Chago and Crayler escorted the vanguard across. Alamo and Pete waded in and swam their horses about thirty yards downstream to head off any cows carried away by the current.

The first cows, sleekly wet and shiny in the morning brightness, clambered up the opposite bank. There Thurman and Daffern waited to drive them out of the way. Prentiss kept them moving toward the campsite.

On the Texas shore, Dusty, Tom Kelly, and Ford Burkhardt drove the cattle forward at a slow pace. Angus wanted no more than fifty cows in the water at a time.

I held my horse midstream, slightly upriver from the herd. I was clad in just a pair of pants. The stirrups felt strange to my bare feet. I hadn't ridden barefoot since I was a kid, and then it had been without a saddle.

"Look out behind you!" Angus shouted from the shore.

I was so intent on watching the cattle I didn't hear him at first. He shouted the warning again and called my name.

I turned to see a tree trunk drifting slowly toward me. I kicked my bare heels into the pony's flank and pulled sharply on the bridle. She swam around the piece of flotsam. It was so waterlogged it barely broke the surface. Several branches stuck out from it.

I grabbed a stout branch, and, urging my horse forward, tried to tow the trunk to shore. It might well have still been rooted in the ground.

The drifting tree pulled me in one direction, and my horse carried me in another. I released my grip before I was jerked out of the saddle.

"It's coming, boys!" I warned.

The current sent the trunk in among the cattle and threw them into a panic.

The orderly crossing operation collapsed.

The cattle swam in all directions. Some circled back toward the Texas shore, where they became entangled with oncoming cows that had not seen the tree. But they smelled the fear, and they, too, panicked. Others turned and swam downstream. A few tried to swim against the current.

Several cows were caught by underwater snags of the drifting tree trunk and brayed their distress.

On the Texas shore the cattle kept coming, adding to the confused mass thrashing about in the river. Over the frightened cries of the cattle, I heard Angus bark orders to stop them. But on they came, as unstoppable as an avalanche.

I plunged in among the milling cows, ducking horns and hoping I wouldn't be unhorsed and fall beneath their churning hooves.

Chago and Alamo worked tirelessly beside me. I caught glimpses of Crayler and Pete prodding the cattle on the downstream side.

We pulled the animals around by their horns. We grabbed their long tails and twisted them around in the right direction.

Alamo stood up on his horse's back and leaped onto the back of a nearby steer. He settled down on it, leaned forward, and grabbed the horns. He bulldogged the animal's head around and headed it toward the opposite bank.

"Heeeee yaaaaah!" He yelled his lungs out. The cow swam strongly toward the shore. Other cattle began to follow in its wake.

By backbreaking work and foolhardy effort, we got the cattle straightened out. We were scratched and bruised, but we hardly noticed it in the excitement.

A few beeves drifted far downstream. All we could do was hope they'd make shore.

When the last cow climbed up the bank into Indian Territory, we stayed in the river to help Zack get the remuda across. It was a picnic compared to the perilous hours we had spent in the water with the steers.

Ginger had set up camp three miles from the river. It was midafternoon by the time the last of the cattle reached there. Angus wanted the herd rested after the trauma of the river crossing. We would set out at the crack of dawn for Beaver Creek. It would be easy traveling over the high, rolling plain.

I was black and blue from wrestling with the cattle. I had a number of scratches from the horns. I figured I'd be stove up in the morning. I had the two-to-four watch, and I hoped to grab some shut-eye as soon after dinner as possible.

Angus estimated his loss during the river crossing at a half-dozen cows. But he gave Ginger permission to slaughter yet another for our supper. It was an extravagance to kill a cow on a drive, since most of the meat would spoil before it could be used.

Ginger and Horse led the steer away from the herd so that the smell of blood would not frighten them.

Ginger expertly cut the meat into thick slabs of steaks and roasts. He dredged the steaks in flour and cooked them in suet in the Dutch ovens.

He roasted the onions and potatoes he'd gotten in trade with the farmers.

Like all range cooks, Ginger threw everything into his son-of-a bitch stew but the horns and hooves. He chopped up lean beef, the heart, liver, testicles, tongue, sweetbreads, and marrow gut. He let it simmer for several hours in its own juices, then added onions and a pinch of chili powder.

At supper the cowboys were in a good mood. The tension of the river crossing was behind them and none among them had been seriously hurt. They were also cheered by the feast Ginger had prepared.

"Hey, Ginger," Burkhardt said as he admired his steak, "that Old Stag you cookin'? Figgered after the way he didn't taken the river Mr. Finlay might be glad to be shut of him."

We ate the delicious repast, and our ravenous appetites sent us back for seconds. Ginger had boggy top for dessert, stewed fruit with a biscuit pastry topping. We ate our fill and drank gallons of coffee.

When the cowboys pulled out sacks of tobacco to roll smokes, I was surprised to see Dusty with a sack in his hand.

"Bought it at the store at Red River Station," he explained. "Time I started smokin' like ever'body else."

He fumbled with the bag and paper, spilling more tobacco onto the ground than he got to stay on the paper.

He never would have gotten it right if Alamo hadn't taken pity on him and instructed him in the art of one-hand rolling. The finer points still eluded him, but he got a decent enough quirley to put into his mouth.

Dusty yanked it out immediately and spat out a few shreds of tobacco. A piece of white paper stuck to his lower lip.

Alamo struck a match and held it for Dusty.

He inhaled deeply and leaned back to enjoy his first smoke.

Instead, he went into a coughing fit.

He tried a few more puffs, but all they produced were more coughs.

Alamo laughed. "Reminds me of the first time I tried it. Only I used corn silk. My mouth didn't taste right for a month."

Dusty slinked off to a spot near the fire. He pulled out one of his penny dreadfuls and started reading. I don't recall seeing Dusty try another cigarette the rest of the drive.

Chapter Twenty

At the noon stop a week later Angus called Chago, Alamo, and me aside.

"Boys," he said, as he inspected the sandwiches of cold roast beef Ginger had prepared, "I want you to start riding flankers. I got a feelin' the savages are mighty close. Like to fight shy of 'em, if we can."

Angus wasn't a man to act on groundless fears. I asked, "That just a feeling, Angus, or you seen something?"

"I was up to Walnut Creek, checking on our night camp," he said. "I seen lotsa tracks in the soft ground. Unshod ponies. Some had rawhide shoes. Tracks led off to the east."

Alamo took a bite of sandwich, and with his mouth full said, "Sounds like a Comanche war party. Or maybe Kioway. Them tracks fresh?"

"Not more'n two days at the most, I'd say."

"Coupla herds ahead of us," I said. "Any sign they been hit?"

"None I could see," Angus said. "They'd take the hides, but warn't no carcasses left for the coyotes. Saw plenty of cattle tracks, but none 'em goin' off with the savages."

"*Señor,*" Chago suggested, "maybe they have gone to hunt some other place."

"Don't seem likely," Angus said. "They know the cattle trail as well as we do."

Alamo said, "Why go elsewhere when they got easy pickin's?"

"They'll find no easy pickin's here!" Angus said firmly. "The heathens'll nae take my cattle without a fight! I want every man to carry his rifle from now on. And I want you three to ride scout. The savages are nearby—I want to know where!"

We set up a system of rotation so that all three of us wouldn't be away from the herd at once. Alamo and I drew the first duty.

"You got any preference, podnah?" he asked.

"The Injuns rode east. I'll ride east."

"That ain't very neighborly," Alamo said. "If you meet up with 'em, save some fer me."

We got our Winchesters from the wagon and rode out. I headed northeast so that I could be about two miles out from the herd and about the same distance ahead.

It was a high, rolling, grassy plain broken by a few ridges. I could see for miles. There was nothing on the prairie from horizon to horizon except occasional groves of blackjack oak trees and a few grazing deer. The wind whipped the grass until it rolled like ocean surf.

Still, the Indians could be hiding somewhere. There were enough dips in the prairie to hide a buffalo herd. I rode slowly up the slope of each rise so that I could see over the top without being easily spotted. I took off my hat each time, lest the high crown give me away.

I rode that way for hours, pacing myself to the herd. Several times I caught sight of the long drive. But even when I couldn't see them, clouds of dust told me where they were. That worried me. The Indians would see the dust, too.

At sundown I rode into camp along the banks of Walnut Creek. We'd follow the stream for a while, and our next river crossing would be the South Canadian. Two days ago we'd forded the willow-lined Washita at Rock Crossing. The river had red clay banks, but the north bank had a rock bottom that eliminated any worries about quicksand. We lashed the wagon to stout cottonwood poles and ferried it across high and dry.

We took extra care with that. Nobody wanted the food stores to spoil or to sleep in wet blankets.

The herd was quiet and bedded down when I rode in.

The aroma of supper was in the air, and it mingled with the smells of the herd, the prairie, and the trees along the creek's edge.

Something else was in the air—*mosquitoes!* Every man was swatting at the pesky critters. The cows wielded their tails like bullwhips to drive the mosquitoes away.

"No sign of Injuns," I reported to Angus. "Not hide nor hair, and no tracks, either."

Alamo had ridden in just ahead of me, and he hadn't seen anything, either.

"I suppose I should be grateful," Angus said, "but it's the waitin' that wears you down."

"They's round here som'eres, that's fer sure," said Alamo. "Mr. Finlay seen their sign. I took a look myself. Them's Injun ponies, fer sure."

Angus said, "I'm sending Alamo and Chago on scout tomorrow. Ben, I want you to ride point with Crayler. He'll take the senior position at the right. You take left. Pete'll ride relief."

I heard a buzzing at one ear and quickly cupped a hand to it. I missed the mosquito.

"Be a good idee, Mr. Finlay," Alamo said, "iffen you'd tell the night watch to keep a sharp eye and nose to the wind. Be jes' like them redskins to burn a coupla sacks a buffalo hair. Makes a fearsome stink an' stampedes a herd ever' time."

"Aye, but I'm thinkin' if they hit in force it'll be in broad daylight. Ain't like a superstitious heathen to come at night. More likely at night they'd sneak into camp and pick us clean without wakin' a man. I'm postin' a guard for the camp."

Another mosquito hovered noisily by my head, then settled on my neck. I dispatched it handily. It was going to be an interesting night.

In the morning we wolfed down breakfast in record time and had the herd on the move before the sun was fully up.

Alamo rode east this time, and he had no sooner disappeared over the horizon than he came tearing across the prairie like the devil was on his trail. We didn't have to ask what was coming behind him.

Angus rode just ahead of the herd. Alamo beat a dusty path for him and reined up sharply. Clods of dirt went flying from his horse's hooves.

"Kioway war party!" he cried breathlessly. "'Bout a mile back, and headin' thisaway!"

"How many?" Angus asked.

"Twenny, I reckon!"

Angus rode back to me. "Keep the herd movin'," he said. "I'll pow-wow with 'em, if they've a mind to palaver. But no matter what, keep the herd movin'. I want every man to have his rifle out an' ready. It won't hurt to show 'em we mean business."

Angus rode over to inform Crayler. I drew my Winchester out of its boot. I held the rifle high over my head and signaled with it to the left swing. He in turn passed the message on back.

The Kiowas came over the horizon and made for the front of the herd at a trot. They were armed with an assortment of rifles, lances, and war clubs. The cowboys eyed them nervously and kept the herd moving. Every man hefted his rifle.

The Indians halted about a hundred yards out. Several of them engaged in a heated discussion, with a lot of hand gestures. Several times one of them pointed toward the cattle.

At last one brave, apparently a leader, rode out about fifty yards and waited.

Angus peeled off from the front of the drive and rode back to confer with the Indian. I couldn't see them too well over the cattle or through the dust. But I guessed that Angus's Gaelic stubbornness wouldn't yield an inch.

The powwow didn't last long.

Angus galloped back to the head of the drive. He didn't give the Indians a backward glance, but he held himself stiff in the saddle.

"It's a fight they want, boys!" he called out. "And it's a fight they'll get!"

Angus had no sooner reached Crayler and Alamo than the Kiowas charged the herd, firing wildly to stampede the cattle.

The frightened longhorns bolted.

We raced beside them, trying to hold them in line. We took potshots at the pursuing Indians, and when we weren't firing, we waved our rifles at the cattle. Several times I sent my rifle butt crashing down on the head or rump of a longhorn that tried to swing away from the herd.

In the melee and confusion, I could hardly see the Indians. But I heard their wild cries and the crack of their rifles.

The rampaging herd swiftly bore down on the chuck wagon. Ginger stood up in front and whipped at Sorry and Sinful. He finally got the wagon out of the way before he was run down.

Chago, drawn by the sound of rifle fire and the thunder of the stampede, was suddenly by my side.

"Take over point!" I yelled. "I'm gonna help Zack with the remuda!" I don't know if he heard me, but he understood my gestures.

The horses were as much a target for the Indians as the cattle. Three braves had gotten ahead of the herd and had nearly caught up with Zack.

Zack, running the horses ahead of the herd, threw lead at the Indians, but they kept gaining on him.

I took after Zack and the remuda, firing my rifle at a gallop. That's something I hadn't done since I rode with Mosby. The art of it quickly came back to me. One brave toppled from his soft pad saddle of cow hide stuffed with buffalo hair.

A second brave spun his mustang around and ran straight at me. He raised his war club over his head.

Our horses collided with an impact that sent both of them down. I flew to the ground and the breath was knocked out of me. Gasping for air, I struggled to my knees and brought up my rifle to deflect a powerful blow delivered by the club.

My fingers were numbed. I swung the stock up into the Indian's belly. He tumbled backward. He was a stock brave with a handsome bronzed face. He was clad in a rawhide breechcloth and leggings. His coal-black hair was parted in the middle and was decorated with a plume of horsehair.

Swinging his club again, he lunged at me.

I threw myself to one side, rolled over, and brought my rifle up. He was on top of me before I could work the cocking lever. The club struck a glancing blow just above my right eye. My forehead went dead, but I could feel blood trickling down the side of my face.

He drew the club back for the death blow. Before he could strike, I rammed a knee into his groin. At the same time I got the other foot under his stomach. With all my strength I lifted him off the ground and threw him backward.

He fell beneath the hooves of the stampede.

In the intensity of our private war, I had not noticed that we had been overtaken by the herd. The cattle thundered by within an arm's reach.

My horse had prudently gotten out of the way and was eating grass thirty yards away. I found my hat and remounted.

Tom Kelly reined up beside me. "Chago seen you was in the way," he said. "He damn near kilt himself gitttin' them critters over."

I was still winded and said nothing.

"You all right, Ben?" Kelly asked. "You're bleedin'."

"Bunged up," I finally managed to gasp. "I'm okay. Les get going."

As we spurred our horses, Kelly said, "I swear this here's as loco as an Irish shivaree. I cain't make heads ner tails who's winnin'."

I said, "That makes two of us."

Once again I didn't know where the Kiowa braves were. There were none on this side of the herd. The dust was an impenetrable curtain covering the running cattle.

I'd been in cavalry battles like this. When you're in the thick of the action, you have only a horseback view of what's happening immediately around you. The overall picture of the battle is simply beyond your ken—and better left to the generals. I wondered if Angus had any better idea of what was going on than I did.

Then it ended as suddenly as it had begun. The noise stopped, the Indians were either dead or gone, and the cattle abandoned the stampede. Better still, we had kept the herd together.

We were nearly to the banks of the South Canadian. When I caught up with Angus, he was giving orders to bed the herd down and make camp.

It wasn't until we sat around the camp fire that night and traded stories that I got a clearer picture of what had happened. Or, at least, as each man thought it had happened.

Daffern said, "I was on right swing. Them Kioway-Apaches come right fer me. All I could think of was I'd never seen the inside of the Saratoga again. I tell you, I could *hear* that orchestra playin'! Next thing I knew redskins was in front a me and redskins was ahind me. No need to aim, just shoot. Reckon I kilt three of 'em. Two fer sure."

Claymore's left arm was in a sling. "I was seein' to the herd an' one a them Kioway snuck up behind me and fired afore I knew it. Blew my Winchester right outa my hand! Winged me a little bit. Ginger done patched it up. Hardly hurts none atall. I got the hostile what done it. Shot him twix the eyes with my forty-four."

As I listened to the stories, I bathed my wound. It was sore to touch, and I had a throbbing ache in my head. I wrapped a clean piece of cloth around my head and counted myself lucky.

Dusty sat in the grass with his supper still uneaten in the plate in his lap. He said, "I never kilt a man before, Mr. Wheeler. Even if it was just an Injun. I was ridin' drag, and one of 'em came back and tried to cut out some of the herd. I couldn't let 'im steal none of Mr. Finlay's cattle. He was dependin' on me."

"You did the right thing, Dusty," I said. "You behaved like a man."

Zack said, "Never was much wif a gun. Kep on a-shootin' at that red man and kep on a-missin'. Lucky fer me he warn't no better shot likewise. He got in 'mongst the horses and made off wif five. But I saved yore night mount, Mr. Wheeler."

We ate beans and biscuits and bacon that night, and we were grateful for even that. If Ginger hadn't gotten the wagon out of the way, our bellies'd be hugging our backbones before we got to Kansas. The stampede would have demolished the wagon—and surely killed Ginger and Horse.

Over coffee, Angus said, "We'll count the cattle in the morning before we cross the South Canadian. I figger the savages got away with thirty head. That an' the horses."

"Been talking to the boys," I said. "Sounds like we gave them Kiowas a licking."

Angus snorted. "I wouldn't put much stock in camp fire talk. I questioned every man, and when I got through I counted more dead savages than they had in the whole war party. Nae, I think maybe we got five or six, and the rest got away with enough cattle to keep their bellies full for quite a spell."

I sipped my coffee and played with the thought that an Indian raid was just another part of life on a drive. Life still went on. At midnight I'd have to saddle up and ride guard. I was glad that Zack had saved my night mount. Finally I said, "I don't think they'll be back."

Angus said, "We've seen the last of 'em. But if they should be foolish enough to come back, we'll fight 'em again. I stand up for what's mine, and no man's goin' to take what's mine without payin' a price in blood.''

He paused for a long time, then said, "I don't have to ask if you feel the same. You been done a terrible wrong. There's men down the trail who got a debt to pay to you."

I didn't say anything. I studied the bottom of my coffee cup.

Angus spread his hands and continued. "I know, I know," he said. "I tried to talk you out of it. Not because I don't think you have a right, but because I know what it does to a man's soul when he seeks revenge. I've been down that road myself. I've never told you that. Fact is, I never told anyone. Only secret I kept from my wife, God rest her soul.''

Angus looked me in the eye and said, "My father was a miller in the Highlands, in Strath Spey. You should see the Highlands, Ben. God himself had to create such beauty. But such beauty also held within its breast such sorrow. My father had fought in the wars, and he wouldn't yield to any man. I come by that righteously. One day my father got into a fray with the laird over a debt, and the laird's men killed him.

"I was still a bairn, no more than fifteen at most. But I picked up my father's sword and laid low his murderer. Aye, vengeance was mine. I barely escaped the banks of the Spey with my life. I made my way to the Hebrides and signed on a coasting ship as a cabin boy. In Bristol I got berth on an Indiaman, and I was at sea for the next three years. I changed ships a few times after that. That's how I ended up at Galveston. A miller's son and a seaman. I'd never been on a horse before, but I became a cowboy."

I said, "I reckon you did the right thing."

"Right, indeed! And I'd do it again!" He stopped, then said softly, "But it tears at a man's soul. That it does."

I knew he was saying that he understood why I had to do what I was going to do. Four men had killed Abby. One was dead. Three to go.

Later, my head still aching, I tried to grab a few hours' sleep before my watch. I couldn't put Angus's story out of my mind. I kept thinking of my own story and how I came to reach Texas that first time so long ago. I recalled my long trek from Virginia to Louisville, where I met Robbie O'Bannion and the crew of *Maid of Killarney*. The ride down the Ohio and Mississippi on his keelboat was a wild and wonderful adventure that helped turn a lad into a man. I thought of the morning we fought off the pirates, then thought no more, and fell into a deep sleep.

Chapter Twenty-One

Three days earlier we had crossed the North Canadian, its banks lined with oaks, cottonwoods, and thickets of wild plum too green to pick. We waded across the shallow river into upland prairies and turned northwest toward Dodge City. Angus didn't plan to cross the Cimarron until we got into Kansas.

The Cimarron, with its pits of quicksand, was the last obstacle before Dodge. But Angus wasn't a man to lay caution aside.

"Keep a sharp eye out for hostiles," he warned at breakfast. "Liable to be Comanche or Kiowa or Arapaho about. Maybe even Cheyenne."

Angus repeated the same order at breakfast every morning. And we kept a sharp lookout for marauding Indians.

But all we saw were miles of rolling prairie and an occasional prairie-dog town. We skirted the borders of one town to avoid its holes. It took us half a day to leave it behind. Occasionally a little prairie dog perched on the edge of its hole and barked at us. Ginger was under strict orders from Angus to keep Caesar in the wagon.

We were crossing a treeless plain. The Great American Desert, some called it. Ginger had loaded the cooney and the back of the wagon with firewood. But he still had to keep Horace busy scouting for buffalo chips. Even they were becoming scarce.

The cattle grew fat on the tender young grass, and Angus allowed plenty of time for grazing. We stayed close to the North Canadian for a few days, then veered northward again.

Kansas was just over the horizon. I would soon be able to tend to my unfinished business.

I rode at left flank, eating dust every step of the way. A steady wind swirled dust around me and seemed to drive it into every pore. The hot summer sun bathed me in sweat. I was itchy and rubbed raw.

That night I peeled off my clothes beside a stream. My body was streaked with dirt.

Naked as a jaybird, I waded out, threw my arms wide, and flopped back into the cool water. I splashed happily in the water with several other cowhands, then grabbed the bar of soap I had beside my clothes.

"I'm dirtier'n a hog farmer," I said, lathering the soap on thick.

"Lemme borry that soap when y'done," said Daffern, who had settled in the water up to his chin.

As Daffern scrubbed himself clean, he said, "Won't be long. First thing I'm gonna do in Dodge is head fer a bathhouse and parboil myself in a hot tub for about three hours. Then I'm gonna put on some clean duds. And *then* I'm gonna splash on lots a bay rum. I tell ya, Ben, ain't nothin' like a little perfumy water to get the ladies excited. I'm gonna hit both sides of th' Deadline—at once!"

I said, "From what I know about the ladies in Dodge, the only thing that gets 'em excited is the smell of a crisp new greenback."

Daffern laughed. "Soon's Mr. Finlay sells them ornery, critters onto some onsuspecting eastern dude, I'm gonna have me enough greenbacks to excite a lot of them soiled doves. Reckon I oughter have pret' near a hunnert dollars after Mr. Finlay deducts fer my horse an' ever-'thang."

I stood to do much better. The trail hands were riding for thirty dollars a month and found. Zack, as wrangler, would get a little less. Chago and Crayler, at point, would get a little more. Ginger was the highest paid man on the drive at fifty dollars a month. His swamper, Horse, was the lowest paid. I wasn't drawing any pay, but I had added forty-six head to the drive. They were mostly yearlings and calves. Still, they'd fetch a good price.

It'd come to nearly a thousand dollars. The only time I'd ever held that much money in my hands was the time in Colchester when I rounded up a gang of bank robbers and returned the loot to the banker.

I didn't know what I'd do with that much money. I couldn't spend it on Abby. She was gone. There was no pleasure in thinking about it.

Actually, I did know what I'd do with it. I'd spend every last cent, if I had to, tracking down Bill Smoot, Kid Bayliss, and Jasper Rollins.

Like I said, there was no pleasure in thinking about it.

Angus brought in a deer at the noon stop. Horse had picked up some prairie chickens on his buffalo chip expeditions, so we prepared for a feast that night to celebrate our passage into Kansas the next day.

"I bagged that buck in Kansas," Angus said. "I was on a rise, and I could see all the way to the Cimarron. When I looked back, there he was. He was a beautiful sight."

I said, "If some Kansas sheriff comes along looking for him, I think we'll have gotten rid of the evidence by tonight."

Burkhardt ambled over on horseback to admire the deer. "Ya dint see any buffalo, did ya, Mr. Finlay?" he asked. "Cain't 'member last time I laid my teeth into buffalo steak."

"Don't see buffalo like we used to," Angus said. "I remember one drive we had to hold up pret' near the whole day to let a buffalo herd go by. Musta been a million of them. Even had elk and antelope runnin' with 'em. They covered the prairie from horizon to horizon, and still they kept on a-comin'. Only sight I ever seen made a Texas longhorn set up and take notice."

"It were an awesome sight, fer a fack," said Burkhardt. "But 'twix Bill Cody an' them hiders, they done whittled 'em down a mite."

Angus nodded. "Aye. So now the Injuns taken to raidin' our herds instead."

Ginger, his derby set square on his head, toiled over the coals.

He had several venison roasts and prairie chickens going at once, and he was frying venison steaks. Pies of red beans and dried apples cooled on the pull-down worktable. Every now and then Ginger brought an arm up to blot his sweating brow on the sleeve of his soiled woolen undershirt.

"Horace," Ginger said, "put more wood on th' fire an' open me another can a coffee."

Horse reached under the wagon, where Caesar lounged, and pulled a few sticks from the cooney.

"Gettin' mighty low on wood, Mr. Ginger," he said.

"You pickin' bufferlo chips like I tol' ya?"

"Like you tol' me, Mr. Ginger," Horse said. "They be mighty scarce. Cow flops, too, Mr. Ginger. Dried 'uns, that is."

Horse put the wood on the fire, then stood back to watch Ginger. He sniffed the aroma of cooking venison and licked his lips.

"Horace, you fergettin' what else I tol' you to do?" Ginger asked as he expertly flipped steaks with a long-handled fork.

Horse removed his tattered Confederate forage cap and scratched his head. "I picked bufferlo chips like you said, Mr. Ginger. 'Cept I couldn't find too many. An' I put wood on the fire like you said."

"The coffee, Horace! *The coffee!*"

Horse's slack-jawed expression suddenly changed. "Oh, the coffee! Like you said!"

He scampered into the wagon and came out with a can of Arbuckle's finest. He opened the can and poured the beans into the grinder. He turned the wheel for a few minutes, then poured the grounds into the big pot. He filled it with water from the barrel strapped to the side of the wagon and placed it over the coals to boil.

Horse held the peppermint stick in his hand. He glanced furtively at Ginger, who was turning steaks. He started to slip the candy into his pocket.

"Horace!" Ginger scolded, his back to the swamper. "You had the last two sticks!"

"Yes, sir," he answered sheepishly.

"Put it on th' table," Ginger said.

Horse laid the candy on the table among the pies and retreated a few steps. He closely examined the back of Ginger's head.

To himself, he said, "I cain't see 'em, but I *know* Mr. Ginger's got eyes in th' back a his haid. They gotta be there sum'ers."

Chago and Alamo came off guard at suppertime. They spooned beans onto their plates, piled it high with biscuits, and received a thick, juicy venison steak from Ginger. Roasted venison and the stewing chickens awaited them for seconds.

They sat down in the grass by me and dug into their victuals.

"That is a toothsome steak," Alamo said between bites.

"Muy delicioso," said Chago.

"Reckon we'll eat our next supper in Kansas," said Alamo. "I won't be sorry to see this drive end. I'm ready to bend my elbow—"

Alamo suddenly stopped, and with a twist of his head, he directed our attention to the chuck wagon.

Crayler confronted Ginger with his filled plate in one hand and the peppermint stick in the other.

Ginger, wielding a butcher knife, ordered, "Put that back where you found it or I'll chop yore fingers off!"

"Savin' it for yer little pet?" Crayler sneered. "Mebbe somebody else got a sweet tooth, too."

"Mebbe somebody's gonna be missin' a few fingers, too!" Ginger warned.

Crayler looked around to assure himself that Angus had not returned from the herd. Emboldened, he said, "Reckon I'll keep it."

I was happy that Dusty was on guard with the herd and not in the middle of another fracas with Crayler. I'd warned Crayler, but I didn't fancy having to shoot a man over a piece of candy.

Ginger drew his knife back. Crayler retreated a step, set his plate on the ground, and took a stance with his hand on the butt of his gun.

"Crayler, I'm warnin' you!" Ginger barked.

"You allus warnin' me!"

Behind Crayler, Caesar darted out from under the wagon and snatched the steak from the plate.

Crayler saw the flash of yellow fur out of the corner of his eye. He whirled, drew his Remington .44, and clubbed the dog across the rump.

Caesar let out a squeal of pain and dropped the steak.

"You son of a bitch!" Ginger swore.

He charged Crayler with the butcher knife raised.

But Caesar, enraged and snarling, turned and sank his fangs into Crayler's leg just above his boot. Crayler cried out in anger.

Chago, Alamo, and I were on our feet, supper forgotten.

Chago said in a hoarse whisper, "The herd!"

Alamo said, "They gonna stampede the herd surer'n hell!"

"We better get to our horses," I said.

We had not moved five feet before the sound of a gunshot split the night air.

Crayler had shot Caesar in the head.

I looked back as I ran toward the remuda. I saw Crayler and Ginger struggling on the ground.

But there was no time for that. The herd was off and running!

Every man not already on horseback was at the remuda. The horses were nervous and milled about. Zack tried to calm them, but several ran off.

Beside the remuda, I saw a hundred or more longhorns thunder toward the camp.

I hurriedly threw a blanket onto the mount's back, hefted the saddle, and pulled the latigo tight. In almost the same motion, I threw myself into the saddle and sped off after the rampaging cattle.

It was noon the next day before we got the herd back together.

The cattle had scattered in a dozen directions. Half of them had run into Kansas, as if they knew the way to market. Some ran back the way we had come from, as if they also knew the way to market and didn't want to go there. Others went east and west.

The bunch I had spied at the start of the stampede had roared right into camp. They narrowly missed the wagon, but they demolished Ginger's pull-down worktable and sent pots and pans flying.

The cattle had run themselves to exhaustion long before the Big Dipper showed midnight. But the problem was finding them in the moonless darkness.

When the first pink showed in the eastern sky, Pete Claymore and I spotted a shadowy mass on the distant prairie. We rounded up about three hundred cows grazing contentedly on the tender grass.

Sometimes we found only a single cow munching on the rolling plain. One by one and in small bunches, we drove them toward the main herd across the border in Kansas.

Angus, speechless with fury, sent us to ride in ever-widening circles until we had found every last beast.

Satisfied at last that we had found all the cattle we were going to find, Angus asked me to ride back to the old camp with him.

We found Ginger and Horse patching up the rear of the chuck wagon with a piece of canvas. Ginger muttered incoherently as he lashed a rope over the makeshift cover.

From horseback Angus silently surveyed the damage. Then his eyes fell upon the mangled remains of a body some distance behind the wagon.

"That Crayler?" Angus asked as we dismounted.

Ginger looked back briefly, then continued his work. After a moment, he answered, "What's left of 'im. Got hisself tromped." Very quietly, he added, "Good riddance, I say."

I heard the final words, but I'm not sure that Angus understood them. He shot a questioning glance at Ginger, but decided not to pursue the matter.

"Foolishness!" Angus swore angrily. He stood staring off into the distance.

"A man killed because of pure tomfoolery! There's no sense to it! Grown men fightin' over a piece of candy! And that dog of yours didn't help matters, Ginger! You agreed he'd be no trouble if I let you bring him on the drive. I swear, I'm tempted to run him off."

Ginger said nothing, but he attacked the rope with renewed vigor.

Horse, who had kept his eyes to the ground during Angus's outburst, sneaked a look at me. Then he looked off to one side of the wagon. I stepped around to see where he was looking and saw a small, freshly dug grave.

Angus came up beside me. He realized instantly that it was Caesar's grave. For once I saw Angus at a loss for words.

I picked up the shovel leaning against the wagon wheel and began shoveling the hard dirt beside Crayler's remains. I dug deep enough to keep the wolves and coyotes from getting to the body.

"Horse," I said, "bring me Crayler's kit."

I spread the tarp and quilts between the body and the grave. I used the shovel to turn the body onto the blanket roll. It was an awful mess. The flies were already swarming. I choked back the bile rising in my throat.

As I turned the body over, something glinted in the sun and caught my eye. It was the broken blade of Ginger's butcher knife sticking out from Crayler's ribs.

I quickly pulled the blanket over it, and Horse and I lowered the body into the grave by the ends of the blanket roll.

Angus took his Bible from his saddlebag and stood at the head of the grave and read several chapters. He ended with a prayer, and I filled the grave.

I said nothing about the knife. I didn't know what could be gained by calling it to Angus's attention. Crayler had been a swaggering bully who was bound to get his comeuppance sooner or later. He provoked the fight with Ginger, and he had killed the only living creature Ginger loved.

I grasped Angus by the elbow and steered him over to the other grave. Angus looked at me in disbelief.

In an aside that Ginger couldn't hear, he said, "You expect me to read the Bible over a dog's grave? That's blasphemy."

I whispered, "You got nothing to lose and a lot to gain."

Angus continued to stare at me as though I had taken leave of my senses.

I said softly, "The way Ginger's carrying on, he may never cook another meal for the Lazy A. I can think of ten ranches that'd snap him up in a minute."

"I—!" Before Angus could protest, I added, "You want to lose the best cook a trail boss ever had? You lose Ginger, Angus, and how long you think you'd keep Alamo and Daffern and Pete? Or any of the others?"

He opened his mouth again. "Humor the man," I said.

Angus sighed and opened his Bible. "I still say it's blasphemy." He leaned closer and said, "Tell a living soul about this and I will skin you alive!"

I signaled to Ginger and Horse to join us.

Angus let the crew rest the remainder of the day. He also wanted the herd to put back on some of the pounds run off in the stampede.

Crayler's death left an opening at point. Angus broached the subject to me, and I quickly recommended Alamo for the job. I had a feeling he was considering me for the job as incentive to ride back to Texas with him.

But I had other matters to attend to when we reached Dodge City.

"Alamo's your man," I said. "He's experienced and he's dependable."

Angus agreed that Alamo had earned it, and he knew he would need an experienced man for next year.

I winked at Angus and said, "Besides, now that Ginger's staying on, I think you got a good chance of keeping Alamo."

Angus looked at me and wagged a finger. "Just one word."

We forded the Cimarron in the morning and moved into a plain thick with grass, goldenrod, sunflowers, and trees with green balls of Osage oranges too bitter for man or beast.

Dodge City lay straight ahead.

Chapter Twenty-Two

We crossed the toll bridge over the Arkansas River and rode into Dodge City along Bridge Avenue.

The Lady Gay Dance Hall was on the right when we got to Front Street. The Varieties Dance Hall was on the left. Across Front, which was a hundred yards wide and bisected by the tracks of the Atchison, Topeka & Santa Fe Railroad, beckoned the bright lights of a dozen or more saloons. The street was so wide it was called The Plaza.

Alamo, Daffern, Chago, Dusty, and I had ridden in from our camp just south of the river. In the morning we'd drive the three thousand head of Texas longhorns into the cattle pens by the Santa Fe.

Tinny piano music filled the night air, mixed with a confusion of loud voices and laughter, the tromp of boots on wooden sidewalks, jangling spurs, creaking teamster wagons, and the crack of whips.

"Ain't it jes' like I tol' ya?" Daffern said proudly. "Streets fulla bull-whackers, hiders, cowboys, and painted harlots. Ain't it a purty sight?"

"Long's I don't have to marshal here," I said. "And I thought Colchester got wild at cattle-drive time."

"You ain't seen nuttin' yet," Daffern said. "They got some new dance all the way from France over at the Varieties. Called the cancan. Ladies throw up their dresses and shake their bottoms at the cowboys."

Alamo snorted. "Only bottoms I seen lately's the back end of a long-horn."

Wide-eyed, Dusty asked, "You mean they show their bottoms? Fer real?"

We laughed, and Daffern said, "Fer real, Dusty. 'Cept they got 'em covered with some kinda lacy pants. Still, it's a sight to make a cowboy's blood pump a little faster."

Dusty whistled.

"What's it gonna be, gents?" Daffern asked. "We gonna watch the dancers or we gonna cross the Deadline and do a little drinkin'?"

The Deadline was defined by the Santa Fe tracks. South of the Deadline law enforcement was lax and things were more wide open. The main part of town, north of the Deadline, was still pretty wide open, but it was more closely patrolled by Marshal Wyatt Earp and his cane-carrying deputy, Bat Masterson. Every cowboy had to check his guns north of the Deadline. But the best saloons—in fact, virtually all the saloons—were over the Deadline.

We settled on the Lone Star Saloon.

Alamo said he would feel more at home starting in an establishment named after his native state.

The Lone Star was one of the smaller saloons, wedged into Front Street about halfway between Bridge Street and First Avenue. At one corner was Charles Rath and Company, and at the other corner was Kelley's Opera House.

Next to the saloon was Zimmerman's Hardware, where F. C. Zimmerman sold everything from pistols to tinware. Sticking out from the false front was a twelve-foot wooden rifle, painted a vivid red and resting over the wide sidewalk on a pole. It was aimed directly at the Dodge City jail and marshal's office, which was in the middle of The Plaza next to the tracks.

"This ain't th' cream," said Daffern, downing a whiskey. "Want th' best, ya gotta go where Chalk Beeson is. He's got hisself th' Long Branch now. We'll mosey over there in a spell."

"Whiskey's whiskey," Alamo said. "Taste's same one place as anothern."

"I'm talkin' atmosphere," said Daffern. "If ya just off a drive and still got trail dust in yore throat, ya in th' right place. Th' Lone Star's a good cowboy saloon. Now, th' Lone Star used to be th' Saratoga when Chalk had it. 'Member me talkin' 'bout it, dontcha?"

Alamo said, "I doan 'member you talkin' bout nothin' else."

"Anyways," Daffern continued, "Chalk's packed hisself over to th' Long Branch—and thas the place you set yer aim fer after a bath and a shave and ya got clean duds on yer back. Whadda you say, Ben?"

"I say I feel nekkid without my shootin' iron. Never been in a place before where you had to check 'em."

Chago said, "A man get a leetle wheeskey in himself, he might feel like he want to shoot up someplace, no?"

"I know," I said, "but I got my eye peeled for meeting up with a few gents."

"Si, the three *hombres* you speak of. May you have good hunting."

Alamo slapped the bar and said, "Barkeep, another toddy."

The barkeep was a round-faced man with a huge black, bushy mustache. He wore a brocaded vest and had frilly black and white garters on his sleeves.

I pushed my glass to him for a refill and asked, "Fella named Bill Smoot ever come in here?"

He poured my drink silently.

I added, "He's a big man, with a nose like—"

"I know what he looks like," the barkeep said.

"Seen 'im lately?"

He studied me for a while, his eyes like black stones. Finally he said, "Who's askin'?"

"A man who wants to know."

He said nothing.

"Man doan seem too friendl—" Alamo said, but I waved him down. It was up to me.

"Name's Ben Wheeler. I run into Bill once in Texas. Thought I'd renew the acquaintance."

I sipped my whiskey slowly. I stared at those black eyes, but I couldn't read any response. He had played this game before.

The barkeep took a swipe at the bar with his towel.

"I reckon he been in town a time or two," he said. "Maybe two, three weeks back. Ain't seen 'im since."

"He with the Kid? Name of Bayliss. Had blue eyes like—"

"I know the one," he said. "Got a mean streak widern Th' Plaza. Nervous fella. Eyes always shiftin'. Allus lookin'."

"He leave with Smoot?" I asked.

"'Spect he's round."

The news struck me hard.

Kid Bayliss was in town!

I could feel my heart pounding in my chest. I tried not to betray my feelings to the barkeep.

I asked, "What about a gambler named Jasper Rollins?"

The barkeep's eyes narrowed. He took another nervous swipe at the bar with his rag. "I reckon you ask too many questions."

We hit the Long Branch next, which was identified by a longhorn's head over the front entrance. Inside it lived up to Daffern's advance billing. The saloon was a long, narrow room, with a gambling room beyond it. The imported bar was ornately carved. Behind it was a huge mirror, and above that was a set of longhorns.

"What'd I tell ya," Daffern said. He pointed to the rear of the saloon. "That's Chalk playin' th' fiddle. The one with th' big mustache."

We all looked. Dusty said what we were all thinking: "They all got big mustaches."

"The one on the right."

The little orchestra played under a stuffed elk's head hanging on the wall. The band consisted of two violins, a trombone, cornet, and a piano. They were playing a sweet rendition of "Lorena."

I didn't learn much more at the Long Branch.

The barkeep hadn't seen Smoot in a couple of weeks, either. He thought maybe Bayliss was still in town, but he wasn't sure. When I tried to question him about Rollins, he told me to ask Luke Short, who ran the gambling concession at the Occident.

We wandered over to the Occident. Short was happy to see me when he thought I was going to part with some of my trail money.

As soon as I asked him about Rollins, his memory suddenly went blank.

I got the impression Jasper Rollins had a few friends in town. And they were covering for him.

After midnight, we collected our guns and led our horses back across the Deadline to the Elephant Livery Stable. The action in the Varieties was still going strong as we passed it.

Dusty, a newcomer to drinking, was unsteady on his feet. We had to help him along.

He looked up at the big elephant painted over the double doors of the livery stable.

"Thash un elephant!" he slurred. "I seen th' elephant once—when I kilt that Injun!"

Inside, the proprietor, Ham Bell, offered us glasses of buttermilk. He regularly walked the streets of Dodge with a bucket of buttermilk, offering a dipper to every drunk he encountered.

Dusty eagerly sipped the white liquid, then spit it out.

"Buttermilk!" he stammered. He clamped a hand to his mouth and ran off into a darkened corner of the stable.

I pushed Dusty's head into a horse trough until he felt sober enough to climb the ladder to the hayloft and sleep it off.

Ham Bell's hayloft was the busiest cowboy "hotel" in Dodge—and the cheapest. It didn't cost a dime.

Chapter Twenty-Three

The next days were busy ones as we moved the cattle into the pens by the railroad tracks.

After some haggling, Angus got top dollar for his cattle. He immediately paid off each cowboy and gave him a horse. Then he sold off the remuda.

Angus paid me for my cattle, then tried to pay me wages. I wouldn't accept the money. I had agreed to do it for no wages.

"You drive a tough bargain," Angus said. "So I tell you what—I'll buy you dinner tonight at Delmonico's."

"That I'll take," I said.

I met Angus in front of the Dodge House, and we walked next door to Delmonico's. The sign in front said: *"The restaurant of the elite."*

"You checked into the Dodge House yet?" I asked as we ordered whiskey at the bar.

"Aye," Angus answered. "And a lucky man I am. I only have to share my room with three other drovers. You'd think for a dollar and a half a day a man could have a little privacy."

"I thought it was crowded in Ham Bell's hayloft."

"At least you can get a man's drink here," he said. "Over at the Great Western Hotel Doc Galland and his missus run a dry place. Not a drop. Man's not only a teetotaler, he don't want anyone else to indulge."

Laughing, I said, "That sounds like old Ham. Every time I run into him he tries to pour buttermilk down my gullet."

"That the fella walks up and down The Plaza with a bucket?"

I nodded, and Angus added, "Talk is he's plannin' to run for sheriff of Ford County. Heaven help Dodge if they get one of them prohibitionists in there."

We picked up our drinks and followed a waiter to our table at the back of the crowded restaurant.

"Charlie Heinz sets a toothsome spread," Angus said as we dug into the meat and potatoes.

"Reminds me," I said. "You and Ginger patched things up yet?"

Between bites, he said, "'Bout as well as you can ever patch up anythin' with that ornery old cuss."

Later, over coffee and berry pie, Angus said to me, "Don't look around but that man at the corner table hasn't taken his eyes off us the whole meal."

I said, "I see him. That's Doc Holliday. Calls himself a dentist, but mostly he's a gambler and gunfighter. One of the best. He and Wyatt Earp're thicker'n thieves."

"Looks a mite drawn to me."

"Too much hard living. The consumption don't help, either."

Angus said, "He's comin' this way."

Holliday, in a long gray coat, black striped pants, white shirt, and string tie, stopped at our table. He was very slender, and his mustache drooped down his thin face.

"Evenin', gents," he said. He looked at me and asked, "You the Texan what's been askin' after that road agent Bill Smoot?"

I looked up at him. By force of habit, he drew his coat away from his right side. But he, too, had checked his gun.

I said, "I made a few inquiries."

"You got business with him?"

"I got some unfinished business he started down in Texas."

"So I hear," Holliday said, then coughed into his handkerchief. "Mind if I sit a spell?"

Before I could answer, he pulled out a chair, spun it around, and straddled it with his hands resting on the chair back.

"You acquainted with Smoot?" I asked.

"I got no quarrel with him, long's he conducts his trade somewheres else."

"He been practicing lately?"

Holliday coughed again. "Maybe. I hear he's developed an interest in railroads."

I digested that information and stored it for future use.

"He been traveling with a fella name of Kid Bayliss? Or a gambler named Jasper Rollins?"

"Bayliss is bad news. Smoot was smart to get shut of him. I seen him struttin' round town. But he gives me a wide berth."

"And Rollins?"

"Played a few hands with him," said Holliday. "Seems Jasper's got a weakness for a holdout, but I keep him honest. He had the gamblin' concession at the Alamo."

"Had?"

Holliday said, "Luke Short's the wrong man to ask about Jasper. Two birds of a feather. Luke suggested to Jasper that the climate here'bouts was gettin' unhealthy. He lit out of town a day or two ago."

"He suddenly develop an interest in railroads, too?"

"Well, he did leave town on the Santa Fe," Holliday said. "But if I know Jasper he probably headed for his old stampin' ground. He's kinda partial to fleecing cotton planters on the riverboats."

Holliday stood up and shoved the chair back.

"Nice talkin' to you, gents," he said. "If you ever got need of a dentist, I got me an office up in room twenty-four of the Dodge House. Satisfaction guaranteed or your money back."

Holliday walked toward the door, then looked back and said, "'Bout that unfinished business—good luck. Never could abide a man with a weakness for a holdout."

Two nights later I was drinking at the Long Branch with Dusty and Alamo. Beeson's little orchestra was playing, and from the next room came the sounds of gambling.

Alamo was angry. "You mean that Luke Short fella up and warned Rollins and he skipped out?"

"That's about the size of it," I said.

"I got half a mind to call him out," he said.

Dusty wanted to march over to the Occident and take a swing at Short. I calmed them both down and ordered another round of drinks. Dusty was sticking to beer and getting more control over his stomach.

"Leastways," Alamo said, "he oughta be horsewhipped. Them tinhorn gamblers stick together, thas a fack."

Dusty was more impressed that I had talked to Doc Holliday.

"I seen him on the street, but I ain't worked up courage to say hello," said Dusty. "Saw Wyatt Earp, too." Dusty opened his shirt front, where he had several dime novels. "I got books tell all 'bout their exploits and adventures."

I said, "I'll find Rollins—and Smoot—when the time comes. Right now, Bayliss seems to be hereabout, but he's making himself mighty scarce."

"The mess of 'em sounds like a prize crew," Alamo said. "You need any help, you let me know."

"Yeah," said Dusty, "me, too."

"Appreciate the offer," I said, "but this is kinda personal."

I finished my drink and said, "Now if you boys'll excuse me, I think I'll head back to my private room at Ham Bell's horse hotel."

Dusty said, "Gosh, Mr. Wheeler, you got that money fer them cows an' all. I figgered you'd move into the Dodge House with th' gentry."

"Dusty," I said, "I'd rather share a hayloft with a bunch of cowpokes than a bed at the Dodge House with four gentlemen. 'Night."

The air was hot, and even at this late hour teamster wagons piled high with hides kept the dust swirling on the bone-dry street. A steady wind off the prairie picked up the dust, along with the smell of the hides, the sweaty teamsters, and horse flops all over the street, and blew it right into my face.

I checked my gun to see that it had five rounds, then set out across Front Street at its intersection with Bridge Avenue.

I stepped onto the board sidewalk in front of the Varieties.

CRACK!

A bullet thudded into a wooden porch post near my head.

I drew my gun and threw myself behind one of the big water barrels squatting outside the dance hall. The shot came from nearby, but there was no sense throwing lead blindly.

The only thing I knew was that it wasn't a stray shot. Somebody had meant it for me.

I studied the shadows. I couldn't see anything. A few curious men poked their heads out of the dance hall. They ducked back in quickly when they saw me crouching behind the fire barrel with a gun in my hand.

The music and revelry continued unabated.

In Dodge it was just another shooting. Killings were so frequent in the wild cow town that people just ran for cover and, when it was over, went back about their business. Dodge was about to have another man for breakfast. I didn't intend to be the man they carted off to Boot Hill in the morning.

I reached down and unstrapped my spurs. Their jangling was too much of a giveaway.

It was my guess the shot came from the direction of the livery stable, just a few doors west of the dance hall. I still couldn't see anyone.

A teamster wagon came lumbering along Front, heading west. I darted out into the street and put the wagon between myself and the stable.

I walked along beside the wagon until I could see the elephant sign. I let the wagon roll past and ran for the windmill and water tower beside the barn.

The explosion of a gunshot split the air. The bullet kicked up dust by my feet. I had seen the flash of gunpowder.

The man was on top of the water tank.

I fired once on the run and sought protection in the shadows of the windmill. Above me the big fan spun rapidly in the wind. The shaft running down the middle of the windmill creaked and squealed as it pumped water from deep beneath the earth.

I studied the water tower. The wooden tank was on stilts and high enough for a man to walk under. The top of the tank was probably fifteen feet high. A ladder was nailed to one side of the tower.

"Bayliss!" I called. "You dirty sneak! I'm comin' after you!"

I kicked the bottom rung of the ladder, gave it a good shake, then ran under the tank and came out behind it. I had a clear view of the top.

I saw a figure silhouetted against the starlight lean over the top of the tank and aim his gun down the ladder.

I fired one shot.

The man grunted, discharged his pistol into the ground, and toppled over the side. He landed heavily by the foot of the ladder and lay still.

I looked around cautiously before turning the body over.

It wasn't Bayliss.

I edged around the feed shed next to the windmill and looked toward the front of the stable. Bayliss had to be nearby.

I worked my way to the door of the stable and peered in. Several lamps cast a yellowish glow, but most of the cavernous interior of the big barn was pitch black. Because of the danger of fire, Ham Bell had only a few lanterns in the stable.

"I'm comin' in after you, Bayliss!" I called.

I threw myself into the darkened barn. I landed on my right hip and shoulder and rolled until I hit the side of a horse stall. A horse whinnied nervously and thumped a hoof onto the ground. The interior smelled of hay and horses and grain and manure.

I looked around the end of the stall. There was no movement except for the stamping of frightened horses.

"Bayliss!" I called.

My answer was a hail of lead.

Bullets splintered the wooden stall. More than one gun was firing. I figured Bayliss had at least two more men with him.

The horse in the stall next to me panicked. It kicked at the side, and each kick sounded like gunfire.

"Texican! You gonna meet your maker!" Bayliss shouted from the darkness.

"That's what you said in San Miguel!" I shouted back.

"I knowed it! When you come askin' for me and Bill Smoot—I knowed it! I shoulda finished th' job when I had you in my sights!"

"I'm here to finish it for you!" I called as I flipped open the loading gate on the right side of the cylinder. I pulled the hammer back two clicks to half-cock. I pushed out the two spent shells with the ejector and slid in three .45 cartridges up to the rim. As a safety measure I always kept the hammer on an empty chamber. I now had a full load of six.

I had to draw Bayliss out where I could see him.

"This the way you settle your quarrels, Kid?" I said. "Hiding in a barn with two men to back you up? I thought you fancied yourself a shootist."

Bayliss quickly answered, "I'm yore match an' more any day, Texican!"

"Bayliss," I sneered, "you shoot women and unarmed men. Doc Holliday knew a *brave* gunfighter like you was hiding in a barn, he'd laugh himself silly. You ain't nothing but a dirty little coward! A yella-bellied, back-shootin' coward!"

Bayliss screamed and fired a volley of shots at the same time.

"You son of a bitch! Kill the bastard! Kill 'im!"

Lead flew all around me. Bullets bit into the wooden stalls and ricocheted off the ground. I hugged the ground and was showered with wood splinters.

The gunfire drove the horse in the stall beside me into a frenzy. It lunged wildly forward, tearing the gate off its hinges.

The horse plunged into the dark area of the barn.

I was right behind the horse. Bayliss hadn't shown himself yet. He needed a target!

I was going to smoke him out!

Chapter Twenty-Four

I ran out behind the horse. I tried to avoid his flying hooves, but I also wanted to stay close enough to deny Bayliss and his friends a clear shot. In a moment the horse would turn and run to the other end of the barn, or a bullet would knock him down.

Either way, I would be exposed to three guns.

At the first shot, the horse abruptly spun around. He nearly ran me down charging to the front of the barn.

I was an easy target, standing in the open center of the stable. There was enough light from the lanterns for anyone to see me. But I couldn't see anyone hiding in the shadows.

I debated. Should I stand and slug it out, or should I do the prudent thing and dive for protection into one of the horse stalls?

It was eerily quiet in the barn after the shot that sent the horse running away. Even the horses were still.

I was in the open. Why didn't Bayliss take advantage of it?

"Bayliss!" I called. "Stand and show yourself like a man!"

In answer, a form emerged from the dark at the back of the livery stable.

I had my gun ready. At least I would get one of them.

The man walked toward me into the light.

Kid Bayliss looked at me and said, "Here I am, Texican."

His gun was in his holster.

Bayliss stopped about twenty feet away. He was shorter than I remembered. His lean body was tense. His right hand hung loosely by his gun butt.

"Where your pals?" I asked.

He said, "Why dontcha ask *yore* pals!"

A voice called from the rear of the barn. "Ben, it's me. Alamo and Dusty. We got his two friends here."

Two men stepped out of the shadows into the light. Their hands were held high and their holsters were empty. Alamo and Dusty walked behind them with drawn guns.

"We heard the shootin' an' figgered you might be in trouble," Dusty explained.

"Came in the back way and found these Jayhawkers tryin' a ambush ya," added Alamo.

"Thanks," I said, dropping my gun back into its holster. "I guess I could use some help, after all."

I turned my attention to Bayliss and said, "Kid, looks like it's just me and you."

He sneered. "That supposed to scare me?"

Even in the dim light I could see his eyes. They picked up highlights from the lanterns. Mean eyes. Killer eyes. Shifting here and there, calculating the odds and figuring how to win an advantage.

I said, "I didn't come here to scare you. I came here to kill you."

"Then les have at it!"

"I'm going to give you an even break," I said. "That's more'n you gave my wife when you shot her in cold blood in that bank in San Miguel."

Bayliss laughed a cheerless cackle. "Reckon you plannin' to talk me to death."

I said, "Grab your piece anytime you feel lucky."

Then I fell silent, sizing him up. I kept my eyes riveted to his. As badly as I wanted him, I wasn't going to go for my gun first. I knew from experience the man who wins a gunfight is the man who takes his time and doesn't allow himself to be hurried.

His eyes gave him away.

I caught the flicker a split second before his right hand flashed to his gun. It was a Colt Artillery model with a five-and-a-half-inch barrel. The shorter barrel made for a faster draw.

He had the gun out of the holster quicker than a wink.

His thumb automatically pulled the hammer back as he brought the gun up. The click was clearly audible. His finger slipped onto the trigger.

The gun arched upward.

It seemed that time had stopped.

My own gun was already in my hand, cocked and aimed squarely at his chest.

CRACK!

My bullet slammed into Bayliss.

His eyes registered surprise. No one had ever beaten him to the draw before.

CRACK!

Eighty grains of lead punctured Bayliss's forehead right between his killer eyes. It blew the back of his skull off.

In a final death twitch, he fired his gun. The bullet thudded harmlessly into the ground.

The impact of my bullets carried him backward. Bayliss landed in a pile of manure.

His two friends were bug-eyed, fearful I would turn on them next.

Alamo, reading their thoughts, asked, "What'll we do with these two bushwhackers, Ben?"

"Turn 'em over to the marshal," I said, holstering my gun. "My quarrel was with Bayliss."

"I never seed anythin' so fast in my life, Mr. Wheeler," Dusty said. "Lightnin' ain't even that fast!"

Alamo said, "Bayliss thought he was fast. There's allus somebody down the trail who's faster. Bayliss met that man."

I remember walking out of the stable and crossing the Santa Fe tracks.

The noise from the saloons and the activity on the streets was deafening, yet I was lost in my own thoughts.

I passed the Alamo, the Lone Star, the Alhambra. I looked in the

Long Branch. Chalk Beeson's orchestra was belting out some tune. I backed out and kept walking.

Finally, after what seemed like hours, I found myself in front of the little Union church on the edge of town. The church was locked. I stood on the front stoop for a long time, just staring up at the sky. A shooting star arched across the sky.

At last the tears came, and I said a silent prayer for Abby. I had killed the man who robbed her of life, but it would never bring her back.

The next day at the Long Branch my money was no good.

If I tried to pay for a round, Alamo or Pete or one of the boys grabbed my hand and said, "This 'un's on me, Ben."

There were plenty of rounds. Dusty's account became more colorful with each telling. And Dusty never seemed to tire of telling it again and again.

"I seen it with my own eyes," he said. "Mr. Wheeler charged into that Elephant Stable with his gun a-blazin'. Them varmints didn't have a chance. It were better'n any dime novel I ever read. Mr. Wheeler traded shot for shot with 'em. He never flinched once. Then he was eyeball-to-eyeball with Kid Bayliss. The Kid had his gun out, but slicker'n bear grease Mr. Wheeler drawed his gun and taken 'im. He put two shots into the Kid. Wham! Bam!"

I protested, but Dusty's embroidered version was accepted as fact.

Dusty and Alamo had saved my life, but neither seemed to realize it. Dusty had me conquering all three men single-handedly. But Dusty himself had acted heroically in entering the barn in the dark, and he wasn't even aware of it. I tried to give him proper credit, but neither he nor anyone else would listen. I'm afraid Dusty had read too many Ned Buntline books.

Chalk Beeson's little orchestra played "Yellow Rose of Texas," and Chalk sent over a round of drinks on the house.

Later, after more rounds of drinks, I noticed Dusty was no longer with us. Concerned that the liquor might have made him ill, I asked Alamo.

Alamo chuckled. "I think he's gone dove huntin'," he said.

I raised an eyebrow.

"Man builds up a powerful urge on the trail," he said. "Even a boy just learnin' how to be a man."

Still later a gaunt man with a drooping mustache, dressed completely in black except for his stiff white shirt, came to our table. He wore a marshal's badge.

"Name's Wyatt Earp," he said. "Like to talk to ya 'bout last night."

Earp and I sat down at a back table, and the barkeep brought us a bottle. Earp poured us each a glassful.

"Just got back from Hays," he said. "Bat told me what happened. Like to hear it from you."

I told him how I had been bushwhacked outside the Varieties and ended up killing Bayliss in Ham Bell's livery stable. I told the story simply, step by step.

"It ain't no secret you been lookin' for Bayliss," he said. "You done ever'thing but put a notice in the *Ford County Globe*. What's your business with Bayliss—and Smoot and Rollins?"

I finished my drink and said, "Back in April, Smoot, Bayliss, Rollins, and Montana Smith robbed the Stockman's Bank down in San Miguel, Texas. I practice law in an office over the bank. My wife had just left my office and went downstairs into the bank. She had the misfortune to walk in during the robbery, and Bayliss shot her in cold blood."

Earp said, "I took him for a no 'count. Never figgered he was a woman killer to boot."

"They hightailed it outa town—but not before I wounded Montana Smith," I continued. "I finished the job on him later that night when we caught up to him holed up in a line shack. To make a long story short, I rode north with Angus Finlay's cattle drive to find the rest and bring 'em to justice. You know I found Bayliss. I'll find Smoot and Rollins, too."

Earp looked at me, then said, "Mighty fancy shootin' for a lawyer."

"I wasn't always a lawyer," I said. "Used to marshal over in Colchester."

His fist hit the table, rattling the bottle and glasses.

"That's where I know your name!" he said. "Been gnawin' at me ever since you hit town!"

I said, "I put my cards on the table, Marshal. How about you? You fixing to charge me with anything?"

For the first time I saw the hint of a smile on his thin, hard face.

"Charge ya with what?" he asked. "Defendin' y'self? Engagin' in a fair fight? If I left it to the town council, they'd probably pin a medal on ya. Kid Bayliss was a public nuisance. Sooner or later he was gonna kill somebody—or git hisself kilt. I might have done the job myself. Word was he already had a couple of killin's notched on his gun butt. You done a public service."

After a moment, Earp added, "'Sides, you can't fault a man for avengin' his family. 's a man's duty. Been my wife, I'd track 'em to the gates of hell—and kill 'em two steps inside!"

I said, "The job's not done. You know where Smoot or Rollins might be hiding out?"

Earp leaned back in his chair. "Rollins I can't help you with. He used to run the three-monte game over at the Alamo. But he skedaddled outa town like a scalded dog soon's he heard from Luke Short you was askin' about 'im. Now that's a piece of work, Luke Short. Too bad you ain't got no quarrel with 'im. Anyways, Doc Holliday seems to think Rollins headed back to the riverboats."

I nodded and said, "Only thing I hear about Smoot is that he's developed an interest in railroads."

"The kind that carry greenbacks in the express car," Earp said.

He spread his hands and added, "But that's outside my jurisdiction. Still, I pick up things. Train was robbed outside of Hutchinson last month. Folks seem to think Smoot had a hand in it. Makes 'em edgy here 'bout. Dodge ain't got no banks. So we gotta send our spare cash back to Leavenworth on the Santa Fe. Mighty temptin' to a man with Smoot's callin'."

As I started to leave, Earp asked, "By the way, what you want me to do with them two yahoos that was with Bayliss? I'd like to hang 'em, but I don't think the judge'd approve."

I shrugged. "Let 'em cool their heels in the lockup for a spell. Then I'd show 'em the county line."

Angus forked another helping of wild pheasant onto his plate and said, "Glad you talked me into eatin' at the Great Western, Ben. Mrs. Galland sets a fine spread. Don't remember the last time I tasted buffalo."

"The turkey's not bad, either," I said. "Wild game's the specialty of the house."

"Tasty," he said, "but I'll be hanged if I'll drink the lemonade."

I smiled and said, "You had a few toddies before I could drag you over here."

Angus put down his fork. I could tell from the serious expression on his face what was coming.

"Ben, about the other night—"

"Angus," I said, "you're heading back to San Miguel in the morning. I hope you're not going to lecture me our last evening together."

"No lecture, I promise you," he said. He picked up his fork and poked at the food on his plate.

"Ben, you killed that fella Bayliss. He was the one what shot Abby. Why don't you come back to San Miguel with me? Pick up your law practice. I'll back you for the legislature. Who knows, maybe you could be in the governor's chair one day."

He shoved the plate aside, reached for the lemonade, and took a swallow. "Look at what you got me doin', Ben." He made a face. "I'm not gettin' any younger. I've got to start lookin' for someone to take over the Lazy A. Come in as my partner. Whatta y'say?"

I thought for a minute.

"I'd say that's a mighty temptin' offer, Angus, and I'm touched. If Abby were alive, you wouldn't have to ask me twice. But you and I are alike, Angus. Neither one of us walks away from unfinished business."

"I figgered that'd be your answer," he said, disappointed.

"After I get this settled—if the offer's still open—who knows?"

Angus sighed. "You said we was alike, Ben. I don't know. I'm leavin' in the morning, and I've got to leave behind some unfinished business."

"What you mean?" I asked, raising an eyebrow. This wasn't like Angus at all.

"Dusty Morgan's not ridin' back with us," he said sadly. "I'm afraid he's fallen into the clutches of a calico queen."

"Dusty?" This was surprising news, but then I remembered what Alamo had said.

It was also distressing news. The hard-hearted harlots of Dodge City were notorious for milking naive cowboys of their trail money—and then dumping them.

"He says he's in love," Angus said. "I say it's just a lot of adolescent moonin' by a lad tryin' to prove his manhood."

I asked, "You want me to look into it?"

"I was hopin' you'd say that. But please," he said, waving a hand, "don't shoot the vanquished virgin."

"Now, look! What—" I started to protest, then broke into laughter. "You old goat! I bit for that one!"

Angus, wiping tears of laughter from his eyes, said, "Let's order some coffee and gooseberry pie, and I'll tell you where to find our young Lothario."

Chapter Twenty-Five

The second-floor hallway over the Alhambra Saloon ran straight from front to back in shotgun fashion. It was illuminated by a single, flickering lantern, as apparently suited its nefarious purposes.

In keeping with that, I had come up the backstairs and jimmied a window to get in.

Angus had asked me to keep an eye on Dusty, and I was not one to stand by and let a friend stick his head into a noose. Dusty was still a naive kid and unlikely to recognize the ruses of an experienced hussy. He would mistake her flirtation for true love.

I was about to give him a rude lesson in love.

Dusty had not hesitated to come to my aid. Here I was coming, unasked, to his. This was much more risky than gunplay. Dusty's pride was at stake. There was imminent danger I could lose a friend.

All Angus knew about her was that her name was Lily Gebhart and that she had a room over the Alhambra.

A few inquiries after I left Angus produced the fact that she was better known in Dodge as "Tiger Lily."

The sobriquet had nothing to do with flowers. Far from being the innocent prairie blossom Dusty thought she was, she was tied up with a tinhorn gambler named Tim O'Rourke. She frequently acted as his shill, and he in turn steered lonesome cowboys into her chambers to be plucked. Once, according to local legend, she had gotten into a knife fight with Squirrel Tooth Alice, and it took five men and six buckets of water to separate them.

I found Lily's room. A faded pick ribbon hung from the doorknob—the signal that she was engaged. I figured I knew who she was busy with.

I knocked on the door. There was a muffled sound inside, and some-one shuffled toward the door.

"Go 'way, can't y'see I'm busy," said a woman's voice from the other side of the door.

I rapped on the door again, this time more insistently.

"Whatta y'want?" the voice said irritably.

"Tim sent me," I answered.

After a silence, she said, "I said I was busy!"

"Tim suggested you oughta see me," I said, getting more insistent. For good measure, I added, "I just sold my herd of five thousand long-horns, and I'm lookin' for some fun."

A key turned in the lock and the door opened a crack. Tiger Lily peeked through. She had mouse-brown hair, pouting lips, and a gold front tooth that gleamed when she opened her mouth. She wore a cheap, frilly wrap in a bilious shade of yellow.

"Tim sent ya?" she whispered.

I nodded.

"Y'say ya just sold yer herd?"

"That's right. I'm loaded and lookin' for some fun." I winked broadly. "Know what I mean?"

She smiled coyly and said in a hoarse whisper, "I'm innertainin' a frien' right now." She hesitated. "Jes' sold yer herd, huh? Why dontcha wait in the bar, sugar. Gimme few minutes to git ridda my frien'. Then come on back and I'll show you what a good time's supposed to be."

I grinned and said I'd be back in a few minutes.

She closed the door. I looked down both ends of the hall. It was empty. A few doors down, toward the stairway to the bar downstairs, was a vestibule where I could wait for Dusty. If I knew Dusty, he wouldn't be devious enough to sneak out the back entrance.

* * *

I didn't have long to wait. Tiger Lily was obviously well practiced in the art of giving cowboys the bum's rush.

I was flat against the wall, and in the dark Dusty didn't see me as he walked past.

I reached out of the vestibule and caught him by the arm. "Dusty, fancy meetin' you here!"

He jumped from surprise. "Mr. Wheeler! I never expected to see—I mean—I—"

He dissolved into mute embarrassment.

"Dusty," I said cheerfully, "no need to blush. You're a man now, and you've got a man's needs. Been visiting your girl, huh?"

"I—how did you know?"

"Just a lucky guess. But ain't you leaving kinda early? It's still the shank of the evening."

"Well, I was gonna stay longer, but Lily—that's my girl—she got called out by the doctor."

"Doctor?" I questioned. "I hope she's not sick."

"Naw, nothing like that. Lily does nurse work for the doc. He came to the door minute ago and said this old lady was doin' poorly and he needed Lily to sit up with her."

"And she couldn't say no."

"Yeah," he said proudly. "She's right public spirited."

I said, "Tell me, Dusty, you still got any money on you?"

"Sure. Got my wad right here." He took the roll of bills from his vest pocket. It was tied with a leather thong.

Maybe I was wrong. Still, I doubted that Lily had changed her spots. On a hunch, I said, "Open it up, Dusty. Let's see the color of your green."

"Huh?" He hesitated, then untied the thong as he said, "See Mr. Wheeler, it's all right here—"

He stopped suddenly and blanched.

A single dollar bill was on the outside of the roll. The rest was nothing but cut paper.

"I had it all!" Dusty said in disbelief. "I had seventy-two dollars left! I counted it all before I went upstairs. I like to count it 'cause I never had so much money before in my whole life. It's all gone! Where could it have gone, Mr. Wheeler?"

"Maybe you dropped it in Lily's room," I said, leading him back to the door. I signaled him to stand out of sight against the wall and be quiet. He gave me a questioning look but obeyed as I rapped lightly on the door.

Lily opened the door a crack, peered out, then opened it wide. "Well, Mr. Cattleman, I told you it wouldn't take long." She had one of those get-rich-quick grins on her face.

"Who was your friend?" I asked casually. "Anybody important?"

"Important!" she hooted. "Don't make me laugh!"

I stepped inside the room, but not far enough for her to close the door. I said, "I'm here to have some fun."

"That's what I'm here for, to show a gentleman like you a good time."

Dusty stepped behind me, a hurt expression on his face.

"Lily," he pleaded, his voice cracking with emotion, "you said you was goin' to sit up with a sick old lady!"

"What's that snot-nosed kid doin' back here?" she exploded. "Throw 'im out!"

"Lily!" he cried.

Then a sudden realization came over him. "My money! You stole my money!"

"I doan know what y'talkin' 'bout!" To me she said, "Throw that kid outa here and I'll show you a good time!"

"So you can pick my pocket, too," I said.

Dusty said, "Mr. Wheeler, I want my money back!"

Lily's eyes opened wide. "You two in this together!"

I said calmly, "I think you better give Dusty his money back."

"Git outa here, both of you!" she said angrily, trying to close the door.

I stood squarely in the way. I grabbed her wrist and held it firmly. "Lily," I said, "I think the smartest thing you can do is give the boy his money back."

"The hell I will!" she spit, trying to twist away. I held on tightly and pulled her closer to me. I could smell her cheap perfume.

"Lily," I said firmly, "if I have to break your scrawny little neck. If I have to knock out your gold tooth—"

"You wouldn't hit no lady!"

"I don't see no lady. Do you, Dusty?"

"Y'hurtin' me!" she whined. "Awright, I'll give 'im his money back. I'll get it."

I released her, and she went to the dresser and opened the top drawer.

I was right behind her. As she turned, she had a derringer in her right hand. I grabbed it and twisted it out of her hand.

"You bastard! My Tim'll take care of you!"

Dusty said, "Yore Tim better think twice on that. This here's Mr. Ben Wheeler, the man what taken Kid Bayliss in a fair fight. And if he don't handle yore Tim, I will!"

Lily's jaw dropped. She swallowed, reached into the drawer again, and dropped a roll of bills into my hands. I gave it to Dusty, who slowly counted it.

"It's all here," he said finally. "Seventy-one dollars. Plus the one she left me on the roll."

At the door I broke the derringer and dropped its two bullets into my pocket.

I said, "I'll leave your little toy outside. Good-bye, Tiger Lily, it's been a pleasure doing business with you."

"Git out, y'bastard!"

Walking down the hall, I clasped an arm around Dusty's shoulder.

I said, "Dusty, I think you did a little more growing up tonight!"

At daybreak I was in front of the Dodge House to say good-bye to Angus and the cowboys I had spent such a satisfying part of my life with.

I shook hands with Alamo and Pete and Ford and Chago and Ginger and all the rest.

Dusty, I was happy to see, was riding back with them.

Angus grasped my hand. He said. "When you've finished your business, anytime you want to come back my offer still stands. Full partnership."

The wind must have blown something into my eyes. They started to moisten.

Angus said, "Good luck. God be with you." He turned to mount his horse, looked back, and said, *"For auld lang syne'!"*

"More of your Bobby Burns? *'For auld lang syne,'* Angus."

I said good-bye to Dusty last.

"You're a man now, Dusty. Don't ever doubt it and don't ever let anyone tell you different. You proved it on the trail, you proved it in the livery stable, and you proved it last night."

"Thanks," he said. "I know it now. Nobody'll ever have to tell me again."

"I'll miss you, Dusty."

"I'll miss you, too, Mr. Wh—Ben. I'm a man now, and I can call you what men call you. Good-bye, Ben."

Dusty took a white, furry object from his pocket and pressed it into my hand.

"It's my rabbit's foot," he said. "I want you to have it. When you go lookin' fer them other two men, I hope it brings you as much luck as it brought me."

Chapter Twenty-Six

Wyatt Earp rose to shake my hand when I walked into the private dining room at Delmonico's.

"Ben, I'm glad you decided to join us," Earp said. "You know Chalk Beeson."

I shook hands with Beeson, a medium-sized man with slicked-down black hair and a large mustache. His hands were big and still callused from his days as a stage driver in Colorado.

I said, "I think I've spent half my time in Dodge at your establishment listening to your orchestra."

Beeson beamed and said, "I hope you also sampled some of our fine Kentucky bourbon, too."

"That I did."

Earp said, "This is Fred Zimmerman. Runs the hardware and gun shop."

Zimmerman, a burly man with a thick black beard, had a viselike grip. "You need guns or bullets, you come see me," he said in a Prussian accent.

George Hoover I had met when I frequented his saloon and bought a fresh supply of cheroots. Charles Rath, who bought and sold buffalo hides, I knew by reputation. Rath was with his partner, Bob Wright.

The other men in the room were "Deacon" Cox from the Dodge House, A. J. Peacock from the Lady Gay, and Henry Strum from the Occident Saloon.

"Gentlemen, why don't we take our seats and we'll tell Mr. Wheeler why we've asked him here," said Earp.

We pulled up chairs around the table. Beeson poured me a whiskey from the bottle on the table and passed the bottle on.

Hoover, handed a cigar across the table. "I know you like my brand, Mr. Wheeler," he said. "Finest hand-rolled. Imported all the way from the island of Cuba."

"Ben," Earp began, "we got nineteen saloons here in Dodge. They do a hell of a cash business, especially in the summer when the herds come to town. The gamblin' concessions bring in still more money. Fred Zimmerman, Charlie Rath, just about everybody does a hell of a big business. George Hoover here wholesales four, five thousand dollars' worth of liquor a month."

Earp paused to let that sink in. He sucked deep on his cigar and through a cloud of smoke said, "The one thing we ain't got in Dodge City is a bank. Makes it mighty risky keepin' that kinda cash on hand. So once a month we load the money onto the Santa Fe and ship it to a bank in Leavenworth. I think you know that."

"That gets mighty risky, too," said Beeson. "Used to drive a stage in Colorado, so I've had a little experience with road agents."

"Fifty t'ousand, that's how much we sendin' out!" boomed Zimmerman. "Ja, dot's a lot of money! I vouldn't enjoy losin' my share, little as it is!"

"And you want me to ride shotgun, is that it?" I asked without taking the cigar out of my mouth.

"That's about the size of it," said Earp. "We're puttin' the money on the Pueblo Express two days from now. You see it through to Leavenworth, and you got yourself five hundred dollars."

Beeson leaned forward and winked. "You been askin' 'bout Bill Smoot. This might be your chance to find him."

"Suppose it's the James boys or the Youngers?" I asked.

Zimmerman threw up his hands. "Ve still need protectin'. Jesse James, Yunkers, Schmoot, who is carin' who tries to steal our money? They show up, you shoot 'em. It's simple, yes?"

Earp said, "I don't know where Jesse or Frank's at. But I do know

Smoot's been operatin' in this area lately. I know he's got informants in Dodge who tip him off about our money shipments."

"Then he'll know about me," I said.

"Like I said, you ain't exactly kept it no secret that you're lookin' for him," Earp said. "And he sure knows about Bayliss. But I don't think he's gonna know you're on the train. Nobody knows about this meetin' or what it's for except the people in this room."

"Things have a way of getting out," I said.

"Vid dis much money, my mouth is ticka-lock shut," said Zimmerman, making a key-turning movement at his mouth with his hand.

"We'll get you a ticket, and you travel under another name. You can be a drover got business in Kansas City or Leavenworth. Or anything you wanna be."

Earp looked at me across the table. They all looked at me.

"Whatta y'say? You with us?" he asked.

My fist hit the table, shaking the bottle and glasses. "If it leads me to Smoot," I said, "I'll ride the cowcatcher all the way to Leavenworth holding the money in my lap!"

The prairie slipped past my coach window like a passing panorama. A copy of the *Dodge City Times* lay in my lap, but I was mesmerized by the flat plains, the gently rocking railroad car, and the clickety-clack of the wheels over the rough track.

The sun overhead beat down mercilessly on the coach roof and raised the heat inside the coach. But you had two choices. Suffer the heat, or raise the window and eat smoke and cinders all the way across Kansas.

I kept a lookout for Smoot's gang, but after a while my eyes began to weary. The heat also contributed to my drowsiness. Still, if he hit the Pueblo Express, I would know about it quickly enough.

"Ticket, please."

Deep in thought, I had not noticed the conductor coming down the aisle of the coach car.

"Ticket, please," he repeated.

I reached inside my coat and took out my ticket and handed it to the conductor. As I did so, the badge Earp had given me was exposed momentarily. I quickly folded my coat back. I didn't want my purpose known yet. Not until it was necessary.

The conductor inspected the seat number and destination on my ticket. "Leavenworth, eh?" he said. "Change trains in Kansas City." He pulled up a punch hanging on a small chain from his belt and put a hole in my ticket.

My job was to keep an eye on the sack of money locked in the express car. Wherever it went, I went. Hopefully, that would be safely to the bank in Leavenworth.

Most of all, I was looking forward to collecting my reward. Not the five hundred dollars they had promised me—but the satisfaction of a confrontation with Bill Smoot.

The conductor had moved on to the next passenger, but he turned back to me. "Dinin' car's open if yer stommick's feelin' a mite empty," he suggested. "Or y'kin stay here. Sandwich vendor comin' through."

I nodded and said, "Think I'll try the dining car."

I got out of my seat and stretched to work out the kinks. "By the way," I asked the conductor, "what time you got?"

He pulled his big railroad pocket watch out of the vest pocket of his dark blue uniform, flipped open the cover with his thumb, and said, "Twelve-thirty." He closed the cover with a snap. "Railroad time," he added smugly.

The Pueblo Express had pulled out of Dodge City five hours ago. No sign of Smoot yet.

A white-coated steward seated me at a table near the rear of the crowded dining car.

"Last table, suh," he said, and handed me a menu. "You is a lucky gennelman."

I ordered a whiskey and reviewed the situation.

The express car, containing Dodge City's fifty thousand dollars, was at the rear of the train. It was between the caboose, which was the very last car, and the baggage car. In all, there were four passenger cars, with the dining car in the middle. The coach I was in was the last one, next to the baggage car. At the head of the train was the wood tender and the 4-6-0 engine from the Pittsburgh Locomotive Works. The locomotive's function was to pull the train and, so it seemed, to spew choking black smoke and cinders from its huge diamond stack.

A special guard from the Adams Express Company rode with the money shipment in the express car. He was well armed.

So was I. I had my .45 in my holster, plus the Colt Artillery Model

I had taken off Kid Bayliss and two boxes of spare bullets stashed in my valise. My Winchester was strapped to the outside of the case.

I was traveling under the name of Henry Johnson, and no one—at least, I hoped no one—knew why I was aboard.

The last time Smoot hit the Santa Fe, he and his men had stopped the train east of Hutchinson and leisurely looted the express car and robbed the passengers.

The prize was much bigger this time. He was sure to know it was more closely guarded. I doubted he would operate the same way. Smoot was too smart to establish a pattern that could trap him.

"'Scuse me, suh," the steward said. "They's no mo' tables, an' I wuz wonderin', suh, if you'd be so kind as to share yo' table wif, uh, this here young lady?"

I looked up. My right hand was still wrapped around the whiskey glass.

The young lady was about twenty-five. She was elegantly dressed in a baby-blue dress with white trimming. Her dark hair was rolled up and pinned under an elaborate hat of felt and ribbons and dried flowers. She carried a huge cloth purse that matched her dress. She was very beautiful and she smiled beguilingly.

I got up quickly. My napkin ring slid off my lap onto the floor. I said, "It would be my pleasure to share my table."

"How chivalrous," she said.

The steward bent down to retrieve my napkin. As he handed it to me, he said in an aside, "Lak I said, suh, you is a lucky gennelman."

"I was just having a whiskey," I said to her. "Would you care to join me?"

She smiled at me and said to the steward, "A sherry, please."

I extended my hand across the linen-topped table. She accepted it in her white-gloved hand.

"I'm Henry Johnson," I said.

"So happy to make your acquaintance," she said. "My name is Irene Managan."

She accepted the sherry from the steward and asked, "Are you traveling on business, Mr. Johnson?"

"Yes, I am," I said, disturbed at having to lie to a woman. "Been out west looking at some mining property on behalf of my company. Consolidated Industries. We have quite an operation in Colorado."

"How fascinating," she said. "Dear me, I'm afraid I was only visiting my brother at Fort Dodge. He's an officer there."

Over coffee we made small talk and gazed out at the passing countryside. It was mostly bare, rolling prairie. Occasionally we passed a stand of oak and thickets of Osage oranges. Along the streams, cottonwood grew in small groves.

As I finished my coffee, I said, "I've so enjoyed our little conversation, Miss Managan. Too bad it has to end."

She raised an eyebrow. "Does it have to end? The time passes so slowly sitting alone in my coach."

Smiling demurely, she added, "I see no reason why we can't share a seat."

I said, "It would make the time pass more quickly—and pleasantly."

"Then it's done," she said. "Surely, the railroad won't object to a gentleman coming to the rescue of a lady traveling alone in the wilderness."

She offered me a gloved hand, and I escorted her out of the swaying dining car.

"Perhaps we could sit in my coach," I suggested. "It's at the rear of the train."

"A most thoughtful offer," she said. "And, please, call me Irene . . . Henry."

Irene kept questioning me about my inspection trip to Colorado. Fortunately, I had once made an excursion into the territory. But I had gone there to bring back a prisoner, not to inspect mines. My memory was a little hazy. Still, it was enough to satisfy her interest.

I hated lying to Irene. It was the first time since the death of Abby that I had paid any attention to a woman. It was purely in a gentlemanly sort of way. Not only was I still in mourning for Abby, but I certainly was not looking for any side adventures to distract me from my mission. Still, she was a difficult woman to ignore. She sat so close to me that I could smell her intoxicating perfume. Once or twice, as she leaned over me to exclaim at some sight on the otherwise featureless plain, her dark hair brushed against my cheek.

Later, after freshening herself up, she took a long look out the window. "Ohio is such a long way to travel," she said. "I'll miss your company when we have to part at Kansas City."

I murmured something noncommittal.

"I don't know when I've—" She stopped suddenly and looked out the window again. "Why, I do believe we're slowing down," she said.

My first thought was that Smoot had gotten to the engine. But one look outside showed me the real cause.

"We're starting to climb a long grade," I explained.

"How interesting. You mean we can't go as fast?"

"It's only for a few miles."

She smiled gently and said, "Well, if that means I'll have more time to sit here and talk to you, I shan't complain."

I smiled back at her and said nothing.

"Dear me!" she said in astonishment. "We *are* going slow. Those men on horseback outside are passing us by."

I spun around, half rising out of my seat, to look out the window.

Three riders galloped next to the right-of-way. They were swinging in close to grab a handrail to board the train.

Irene said, "Why don't you sit down and relax, Henry. I do believe they're going to rob the train."

"What—!"

I felt the gun in my side.

I looked down. She shielded it with her purse.

It was my gun!

She had taken it out of my holster when I turned to look out the window.

Her thumb pulled the hammer back, and it clicked loudly.

Irene smiled again. This time it was the triumphant smile of a cat.

"Now, just sit back and relax," she purred. "Bill Smoot is just dying to say hello to you—*Mr. Ben Wheeler!*"

Chapter Twenty-Seven

Irene pressed my gun into my side and said, "Mr. Wheeler, I do seem to have the drop on you."

"Yes," I said grudgingly, "and I seem to have been caught with my guard down."

"How embarrassing—for you."

Our voices were normal and calm. I don't think any other passenger was aware of what was happening between us. It probably wouldn't have made any difference. They were already terrified at the prospect of being robbed at gunpoint by Bill Smoot and his gang.

"You are a woman of considerable charms," I said. I wanted to keep the conversation going.

"I guess it was your charm that threw me," I said. "You're much too elegant for Bill Smoot."

She frowned and said, "My only interest in Mr. Smoot is what he can do for my purse. The man is rather uncouth, you know."

"I hope, for your sake, he sees it the same way," I said.

"Our association is purely mercenary, I assure you."

I said, "Now where have I heard that expression before? I know! From a hundred professional women along The Plaza in Dodge City!"

Her eyes flashed and she jabbed the pistol harder into my ribs. "How dare you compare me to those—those—!"

"Painted cats?" I offered. "Perhaps I was wrong. They hold men captive with their charms while they rob them. You would never do that, would you?"

"I am very tempted to pull this trigger myself and deny Mr. Smoot the pleasure!" she said, biting off the words.

For the first time since she had gotten the drop on me with my own gun, I smiled.

I said, "Go ahead, pull the trigger—if you think it'll do you any good."

"What do you mean?"

"Without bullets a pistol is just another piece of iron," I said. "I think you'll find all the chambers empty."

She turned the gun slightly so that she could inspect the chambers. They were indeed empty.

"Damn you!" she cursed. She threw the gun down, seized her handbag, and began fumbling at the drawstrings.

I pulled a tiny derringer out of my coat pocket and aimed it at her. "This what you looking for?" I asked.

"I—you—damn!" she sputtered. "What are you doing with that? Give me that! It's mine!"

"Forgive me for going through a lady's purse," I said, "but I took it out when you went to freshen up. I also emptied my pistol."

"How did you know?"

I shrugged. "I didn't. It's not unusual for a lady to carry a derringer. In fact, it can be downright prudent. But I had a pretty good idea Smoot was going to attack the train. And I also had a pretty good idea he would have somebody on the train to take care of me. Since you seemed to be paying a lot of attention, you were the likely candidate."

At that instant a drunken cowboy, his hat pulled down over his face, reeled down the aisle. Suddenly he threw back his hat, and in a flash had a Remington .44 in his hand.

I nearly shot him with the derringer before I realized it was Dusty!

Irene, reacting to what I had said, spat out a curse. "You bastard!" she cried.

Dusty's jaw dropped as he looked at her. Finally, his voice trembling with shock, he said, "Ma'am, I never heard a lady utter a blasphemous word in my life before. My mother would die of mortification if she even heard such a word. You must be a scarlet woman."

Irene looked at Dusty, then at me. She asked, "Are you sure this one's weaned?"

"Dusty, what the hell are you doing on this train?" I said as I recovered my revolver from the floor and reloaded it.

"Gosh, Mr. Whee—I mean, Ben, I figgered y'might need help," Dusty stammered, starting to blush. "I mean, I loved Abby, too, and I got a duty to perform just like you do. First night on the trail I hightailed it back to Dodge. I left Mr. Finlay a note. I wouldn't want him thinkin' I was ungrateful or anythin' or maybe sneakin' back to see Lily. Then I saw you git on th' train this mornin', so I got on, too."

I shook my head. I wasn't sure if I should be grateful or annoyed. But I was touched by Dusty's concern and his feelings for Abby.

"I seen she had th' drop on you, but, gosh, Ben, I couldn't shoot no lady." His blush deepened. "Wal, I see now she ain't no lady. No lady would say what she jes' said."

"Where'd you get this hayseed?" said Irene, fuming.

I knew I had to act fast. I shucked my coat. Everyone could see the badge pinned to my vest.

I said, "I'm a special deputy marshal and this woman is in cahoots with the gang fixing to rob this train! Dusty, I want you to stay and watch her. I'm going outside."

"I'm goin' with ya," Dusty said. "Y'gonna need help."

"I don't wanna have to worry about looking after you," I said.

I was sorry to hurt Dusty's pride, but I didn't want him going up against experienced desperadoes.

I got my bag from the luggage rack, shoved the extra pistol into my belt, and dumped shells into my vest pockets. Each gun had only five rounds, with the hammer on an empty chamber. I didn't want to risk accidentally shooting myself while scrambling on top of the train.

As I reached the car door, Irene screamed at me, "I hope Bill Smoot gets you! I hope he shoots you dead!"

Chapter Twenty-Eight

I looked through the window in the door at the end of the coach. The platform appeared to be empty. I couldn't see anybody.

Gun in hand, I cautiously opened the door and stepped onto the platform. I was immediately struck by the noise of the wheels on the tracks, and the wind carried wisps of sooty smoke past the car.

I leaned over the side and took a quick look forward and to the rear. I couldn't see anybody in either direction. I tried the other side and still saw no one.

I couldn't even see the riders or their horses. Smoot and his men had to be aboard the train.

Over the roar of the clacking wheels and rushing wind, I heard a noise overhead. I pressed back under the overhang.

A man leaped over the yawning space between the two cars, heading for the front of the train.

I reached around the side of the forward car and grabbed a rung of the ladder to the roof.

I swung out and dangled over open space.

The wind tugged at me, and my feet hung close to the ground rushing past me below. I pulled one foot up, found the bottom rung by feel, hooked a booted toe onto it, and hoisted myself up.

Hand over hand, I climbed up until I could see over the top of the car. I looked first to the rear. It was clear. To the front I could see the man who had passed me a moment ago. Ahead of him was another man.

Their backs were to me. Apparently they were headed for the locomotive to stop the train.

Where were Smoot and his other gunmen? My guess was they were as close to the express car as they could get. I knew they weren't in the last passenger car, which was directly ahead of the express and baggage cars.

So they were probably in the caboose.

The express car was firmly bolted shut, and there was an armed guard inside. Smoot would want to stop the train and take his time breaking in.

My first task was to keep the train moving. That would at least slow down Smoot.

I scrambled onto the top of the car and started after the two men going for the locomotive.

The catwalk running the length of the car was narrow, and the car rocked sickeningly from side to side. I had to lean into the wind, which tore at my clothes and tugged at my body. Smoke and hot cinders swirled around me. They obscured my view of the men ahead of me, but they also gave me some protection.

Between each car was a thirty-inch open space that had to be leaped. One miscalculation and I would land under the train's wheels.

All things considered, I'd prefer to be in the middle of a stampede.

I could no longer see the men in front of me. They'd probably reached the locomotive. If so, I'd better prepare for a sudden stop that could pitch me right off the top of the train.

I hurried to stop them.

I leaped onto the dining car and ran along the raised platform. Two more passenger cars and I would be at the wood car and engine. I had to keep the train moving. I had to keep Smoot off balance.

As I sprang from the dining car to the next passenger car, I could feel the void between them sucking at my feet, beckoning me to destruction beneath the wheels. The track and roadbed between the two cars raced by in a blur.

My high-heeled cowboy boots landed hard, and I fought to keep my balance. The car lurched. I thought at first the two desperadoes had reached the locomotive and the train was stopping. But apparently it was just a bad piece of track.

I remembered the tightrope walker I had seen in that circus so long ago in New Orleans. I kept my arms out, shifted my weight from side to side, and kept my balance.

I was on the forward passenger car. The wood tender and locomotive were directly ahead. I could smell the engine's greasy heat. Its big stack spewed a column of thick black smoke that fell back upon the car in a choking, eye-stinging cloud.

Suddenly, in the swirling smoke, a head rose at the front end of the car.

It was one of the bandits, and he had a gun leveled at me over the roof. I knew it had been too much to expect that I wouldn't be spotted.

CRACK!

A bright orange flame flashed at the end of his gun barrel.

But I was flying forward in a sprawling dive. His bullet whined over my head.

My own gun was out, and I fired two rounds before I landed on the roof of the car.

My shots went wild, but it forced him to duck.

I landed on the car roof with a thud, half on the raised walkway, half off. The extra gun tucked into my belt bruised my stomach.

I clung to the top of the rocking passenger car. It would be a simple matter to lose my grip and go sliding off the sloping side.

My .45 was aimed where I guessed the man's head would appear.

He didn't show himself.

I waited a moment longer. He still didn't appear, and I began to grow uneasy.

Suddenly shifting my weight, I rolled over onto my back. I brought my gun down and aimed it toward the rear of the car.

Paydirt! The man had apparently run through the passenger car to get behind me.

CRACK!

A ball of lead gouged out a shower of splinters where I had been a moment before.

The man was climbing onto the roof of the car.

I fired two quick shots. Then another.

He loosened his grip on his gun, and it twirled on his trigger finger. His eyes opened wide in surprise and fright. Then he fell, clinging desperately to the sloping edge of the roof. The scream that escaped his throat was unearthly. His fingers clawed at the roof, but they could find no purchase. He slid off into oblivion.

It wasn't the same bandit who had fired at me from the front of the car. They were trying to catch me in a crossfire!

I rolled back onto my stomach.

The other bandit was standing up in the swaying wood tender, trying to steady himself long enough to take aim.

I swung up my pistol, cocked it, and squeezed the trigger.

There was a click as the firing pin struck the empty chamber.

Damn! There wasn't time enough to get the extra gun out. But I was going to try anyway.

I saw the bandit aiming at me.

I was still pulling the gun from my belt.

Everything seemed to slow down.

I heard the explosion of gunfire!

He couldn't miss at that range. I would soon see Abby again.

Instead, the bandit threw his arms wide, his head flew back, and he toppled backward out of sight.

"You awright, Ben?"

I turned to see Dusty emerging from the smoke. His gun was in his hand.

"I'm sorry," he apologized. "I dint mean to shoot him before you could, but I dint like the way he was aimin' at ya."

"Dusty," I said as I got to my feet. "You saved my life again! I was out of bullets."

"Gosh! You mean y'ain't mad 'cause I shot 'im 'fore you could?"

"Mad? I love you!"

"Wow!"

I wasn't going to get caught short again. I loaded both guns with six rounds.

The bandit Dusty killed was sprawled on top of the wood car.

Dusty turned pale when he saw him.

"I never kilt nobody before," he said. "'Cept that Injun. My stomach doan feel good."

I said, "I hope you never feel good about killing a man, Dusty. But sometimes it's necessary. You saved my life, remember that."

He wiped his nose on his sleeve. "I know," he said, choking back a sob. "I'm right proud I saved yore life. But killin' a man's nothin' I'm ever gonna brag on."

"I think you got the right idea," I said.

I hailed the fireman as I leaped into the tender. Dusty jumped down behind me.

He threw up his hands and cried, "Don't shoot, mister!"

I pointed to the badge pinned to my vest.

The fireman started to lower his arms, but he wasn't sure. The engineer looked back nervously. He kept one hand on the throttle.

"Special deputy," I said loudly over the noise of the huffing, puffing engine. "Marshal Earp in Dodge City sent me to guard the money shipment in the express car."

The engineer touched two fingers to the bill of his striped cap. "Damned if y'ain't doin' a good job of it!" he said. "I seed you send them two varmints to glory!"

The engine cab was hot and noisy and had a sulfurous smell to it. Tiny fingers of flame licked at the grate of the firebox.

"You better throw on some more wood," I said. "Don't stop this train for nothing. I'm going back to the express car to see what I can do about the others."

I put a hand on Dusty's shoulders. "This is Dusty Morgan," I said. "He took care of that second desperado. Dusty's going to stay up here and see that nobody else tries to stop the train."

I climbed back onto the wood tender. "Keep 'er moving, no matter what!"

The fireman said, "Y'gonna go back there to save *their* money? You must be gettin' a nice reward."

I said, "Money's got nothing to do with it. This is strictly personal!"

Chapter Twenty-Nine

I was too late as I ran across the top of the baggage car.

The express car had been cut loose and was drifting away, inch by inch. Smoot's men had uncoupled it, and on the uphill grade gravity was starting to exert its pull.

The two cars were too far apart for me to leap to the roof.

But if I acted fast I might be able to reach the platform railing.

The iron railing did not extend all the way around the platform. It had openings for passengers to board on each side and an opening at the front for passengers to go from one car to another. But there was still plenty enough to grab on.

I gave one final shove with my foot. The momentum carried me out into the open space between the two cars.

I was flying toward the express car, which was still rolling forward. Yet I felt suspended in midair. Would I make the connection, or was fate awaiting me beneath the wheels?

My fingers were only inches from the top of the platform railing.

It seemed an eternity before I closed the distance.

My fingers clamped tightly over the iron bar.

My feet swung down and would have hit the roadbed if I hadn't pulled them up. I hit the front of the platform with a force that nearly took my breath away.

I struggled to pull myself up.

It was then that I saw the bandit.

His hands were on the big brake wheel on the other side of the platform. He was tightening the brakes to halt the express car and caboose.

He was as surprised to see me as I was to see him. He gaped at me for the longest time, his hands still on the brake.

Before he recovered his senses, I was nearly onto the platform.

"What th' hell!" he gasped. The last thing he expected to see was somebody from the departing train come flying through the air.

He lunged at me and tried to pry my fingers off the railing.

I had one leg hooked over the coupling and the other on the platform. I kicked at him desperately. My booted toe caught him just below the knee. He cried out in pain and stumbled back.

It was time enough for me to drag myself onto the platform at the walk-through.

I grabbed the train robber by one boot and jerked hard. He lost his footing and fell.

As I charged him, he kicked me in the face and I tasted blood in my mouth. He kicked again, and I ducked. His boot scraped along the side of my head. It hit my ear so hard I thought it had been torn off. It hurt like hell, then began to feel numb.

I grabbed his boot with both hands and twisted with all my strength. He rolled onto his stomach or I would have broken his ankle. He wouldn't walk on that foot for a while without remembering me.

I got my knees under me, then partially raised myself up. Bracing myself with one hand on the railing, I put a foot against him and shoved him toward one side of the platform. I was going to push him through the passenger entryway.

I'd nearly gotten him off, but suddenly he grabbed a railing post and held on for dear life. His knees were on the steps.

I smashed his hand with my boot, gave him another kick, and he fell off the car.

He tumbled several times in the dust, then lay still.

The express car, with the caboose still attached to the rear, gradually came to a halt.

I loosened the brake. Gravity exerted its pull once again, and the cars slowly began to roll backward down the grade.

That ought to give Smoot pause.

I banged on the door to the express car with the butt of my gun, then stood aside.

A rifle slug plowed through the thick wooden door. It sent a plug of wood flying.

"I ain't openin' up," the guard inside yelled.

"Special deputy from Marshal Earp!" I said.

"That's what *you* say!" the guard answered. "I still ain't gonna open the door!"

"I *want* you to keep the door locked!" I said. "I just want you to know I'm here!"

"Earp said he was puttin' a special deputy on the train! Mebbe it's you and mebbe it ain't. But I doan aim to open up to find out!"

I said, "You stay locked inside! I'll take care of things out here!"

The two cars picked up speed as they rolled back down the grade. We were going down faster than the locomotive had pulled us up.

I climbed up the ladder and peered over the top of the express car roof.

Someone was standing on the roof by the smokestack. His back was to me, but he was too small to be Smoot. Dusty and I had already taken care of three of his men. It had to be just this man and Smoot.

I made my way onto the roof. He hadn't seen me yet. I had my gun in my hand.

He struck a match on the stack and turned to shield the flame with his body and cupped hand. Something in his hand sparked to life.

He had a stick of dynamite in his right hand, and he was about to drop it down the smokestack into the express car below.

That's when he saw me.

He didn't have time to go for his gun. Instead, he tossed the dynamite to me.

It had a very short fuse, and it was burning rapidly.

I fired and he dropped like a rock onto the roof.

The dynamite stick arched toward me and landed at my feet.

I caught it with the side of my boot and kicked it over the side of the car.

It exploded harmlessly along the roadbed.

At the far end of the express car, an arm swooped up, then disappeared.

Another lighted stick of dynamite sailed toward me.

It landed too far away for me to reach it in time.

I aimed my gun at the dynamite and fired. The stick leaped into the air as bits of dynamite and paper flew everywhere.

The stick landed on the edge of the roof, then rolled off.

A thunderous roar rocked the express car and knocked me off my feet.

I clung to the catwalk to keep from falling off the car. My gun scudded across the rooftop.

I saw the next stick coming. It landed a few feet from my face. All I could see was that burning fuse.

I didn't know where my gun was. There was no time to get the other gun from my waistband. I stared at the malevolent object. The fuse hissed and popped. It was only an inch from the detonator.

The car still reverberated from the last blast. As the fuse burned toward the end, the car lurched and sent the stick rolling down the slope of the roof.

It dropped from sight.

The blast seemed to lift the express car right off the tracks.

It was so close and so loud I thought my eardrums would burst.

Broken pieces of wood flew up in all directions. The blast had taken a bite out of the side and roof of the car.

I was so stunned I wondered if I could hold on. I wondered, too, if the car would stay on the track. I was pelted with pieces of debris. Splinters of wood littered the roof.

Dust from the blast had gotten into my eyes. I blinked several times to clear them. When I opened them again, I saw Bill Smoot walking toward me. His gun was aimed at my head. Dust and tiny pieces of wood from the blast flecked his beard.

I didn't know where my gun was. The blast surely had blown it off the roof. I could feel the other gun, Kid Bayliss's gun, pressing against my abdomen. But how could I get it out?

"Y'sure caused me a peck a trouble," said Smoot.

"Nothing like the grief you caused me," I said.

Smoot laughed wickedly. "I mind th' time y'caused me no lack a grief down near Colchester."

"It wasn't too friendly of you to rob the bank," I said.

"Man's gotta earn a livin', ain't he?"

"You shoulda been a storekeeper."

Smoot shook his head and pursed his lips. "I wasn't cut out fer no indoor work. 'Sides, I had a trade.''

I said, "I guess your trade was robbing banks and mine was chasing after you."

"You shouldna killed Montana," he said suddenly, his voice turning mean.

"Had to," I said. "You killed my wife in that bank holdup."

"Twern't me," he said. "It was that damn fool kid. You done settled it with him."

"Now I'm gonna settle it with you, Bill. You planned the robbery. You brought the kid there."

"You killed Montana. Him and me was like brothers. Closer, maybe."

All the while we had been talking, I had been slowly getting to my feet. But I was still low enough for one hand to reach out behind me and grasp a broken board blown up by the explosion.

"I doan care 'bout the Arkie," Smoot said. "He warn't nothin' but trouble anyway. An' you can plug ol' Jasper fer all I care, too. Bastard even tried to cheat on me at cards!"

He raised up the gun.

"But y'killed Montana. You gonna pay!"

I threw myself forward. At the same time I brought the board up and swung it at his gun. I didn't know if I could get close enough to connect.

The tip of the board hit the tip of the barrel.

He fired at the same time.

I could hear the bullet as it whined past my ear. It was so close I could feel the heat.

I was nearly off balance from swinging the board, but I managed to bring it back up and hit him again. He staggered back a step.

I dropped the piece of wood, and my hand closed over the gun in my belt. In an instant it was out and my other hand fanned the hammer.

I put three bullets into Smoot. He didn't get off another shot.

Smoot slumped to his knees. His hands tried to stem the flow of blood staining his shirt. His eyes clouded over.

He looked up at me and said, "Never shoulda tied in with that damn fool kid!"

He pitched forward and said no more.

That left only Jasper Rollins. I knew I would find him on the river after I delivered the money to Leavenworth.

Chapter Thirty

St. Louis set my mind reeling back nearly twenty years and evoked memories of my arrival in Louisville.

Maybe all river towns looked alike, as did all cow towns. St. Louis had that same endless sprawl of houses and businesses tumbling down to the wide ribbon of dark water.

It had that same panorama of immaculate white steamboats hugging the riverbank like beetles and thrusting up black chimneys like a forest of smoking antennas.

I felt the same pang of hunger I had experienced the evening I fortuitously met Robby O'Bannion in front of that waterfront beanery. Even though my stomach had been satisfied by a repast at St. Louis's most elegant restaurant.

I felt the same sense of desperation I had felt on the Louisville waterfront when I had fruitlessly sought passage to Texas before meeting Robby O'Bannion.

Yet, my mission was nearly over, not just beginning as it was then. Montana Smith: dead. Kid Bayliss: dead. Bill Smoot: dead. Irene Managan was in the hands of the marshal in Kansas City, and Dodge City's fifty thousand dollars was safe in the bank at Leavenworth.

I had only to find Jasper Rollins to complete the vow I had made to avenge Abby.

Find Rollins. I might as well try to guess the number of stars in the sky.

Jasper Rollins was a slippery rascal with a remarkable sense of self-preservation. He had not the pride to stand and fight, nor the courage to face a man down. Jasper Rollins was more dangerous than that.

He was a cornered rat.

By my fourth day in St. Louis, with Dusty in tow, I began to feel I knew the waterfront as well as Pa's bottomland farm back in Virginia. Or my own spread in San Miguel. I had been to every saloon. Several times, in fact. Every cafe, hotel, and backroom gambling joint.

The barkeep chewed on a wad of tobacco that puffed out one cheek. At the same time, he had a matchstick in his mouth. It bobbed up and down whenever he talked.

He made another desultory swipe at the bar with his dirty rag. He spit into a stone jar he kept behind the bar.

"Who's this gent y'lookin' fer again?"

"Jasper Rollins. A gambler, with a red beard—"

"Never hear'd a 'im."

"A red beard, y'say?"

"That's right. Works the riverboats."

The ferret-faced dealer ran a finger around his dirty starched collar and craned his neck.

"Sure you doan wanna play a little keno?" he asked, putting his hand on the pivoting goose that spun around to mix the numbered balls used in the game.

"I'm sure," I said.

"How 'bout yer young frien'?" he asked, dipping his head toward Dusty.

"He ain't interested, either. How about it? Jasper Rollins?"

"I dunno. Them riverboat gamblers doan stop here much. Pickin's too ripe on the river."

The desk clerk gave me a disdainful look through his pince-nez glasses and said, "A gambler? My good man, this is a high-class establishment. I'm afraid we don't cater to the riffraff."

I met every incoming packet boat. I saw every departing one off, which was no easy task in so busy a port.

The steam whistle gave a melancholy blast, and the boat, its lanterns ablaze, backed out into the river to begin its journey to New Orleans.

It was nearly midnight. I had been watching its passengers straggle aboard since nine o'clock. I had questioned the purser. Still, I had no way of knowing whether Rollins was aboard or not.

Dusty had fallen asleep on a stack of grain sacks piled up on the wharf. I gently shook him awake.

"Is it gone?" he asked between yawns.

"You can see it out in the river," I said.

He was too sleepy to look. "Kin we go back to the hotel now?" he asked.

Down the esplanade I saw the yellowish light of a cafe beckoning. I suggested some coffee and a piece of pie. Dusty nodded sleepily.

How I wished Angus was here to share a cup of coffee. I missed the old Scotsman and his wise counsel. I knew what he would advise. I could hear his voice now: "Lad, give it up before it consumes you! You got the man who killed Abby. And you got the leader. Isn't your anger satisfied? Hasn't enough blood been spilled? It's not right to put Dusty in any more danger."

I was sorely tempted to take Angus's advice, even if it was in spirit only. My search for Jasper Rollins was frustrating and disheartening. I was going in circles.

The night was dark and the esplanade was deserted. Huge crates and sacks of grain awaiting shipment were stacked along the broad walkway.

I should have had my mind on what I was doing, not pining for Angus.

Three footpads fell upon us from behind a pile of crates.

One grabbed my arms from behind. Another swung at me with a lead-weighted sap and hit me above the eye.

The third tangled with Dusty, who suddenly became very much awake.

"You ask too many questions!" said the man with the sap. He wore a billed seaman's cap, and he had a jagged scar running from one eye to his chin. This man had been in a few fights before.

He drew back the sap.

I tugged on the man pinning my arms and pulled him around. The sap landed on his shoulder and he loosened his grip. I tore free from his injured arm. I grabbed his coat collar and his belt and swung him around like a sack of grain. He collided heavily with the man with the sap. They both went down.

I turned my attention to the man pummeling Dusty. The man was wearing brass knuckles. Dusty was bleeding from the nose and mouth.

I kicked the man hard behind the knee. That got his attention. As he stumbled around, I kicked him with all my might in the groin. He screamed so loud I'm sure they could hear it on the Illinois side of the river. These men fought the way I had learned to fight on the river with Robby O'Bannion. Gouge, kick, bite, play dirty, and no quarter asked or given.

"Behind ya!" Dusty said, spitting blood.

I saw the flash of the knife in the hand of one of the other two as he got to his feet. He grinned as he rushed at me.

"No more questions!" he said. "Jasper sent us to shet yore mouf!"

He slashed at me with the knife. I leaped back.

The man with the sap fell on me like a bear on honey. I couldn't get to my gun. The shiny blade was poised to gut me.

Whoooooosh! A black lacquered stick arched through the air and landed on the fist holding the knife. The man cried out in pain, and the knife flew away.

Out of the corner of my eye I saw a fourth man, and he was wielding a blackthorn walking stick like Robby O'Bannion with a shillelagh.

Whooooooosh! He cracked the skull of the footpad.

I broke free of the man holding me and drove my fists into his stomach. He doubled over, and I swung my right from the ground and connected with an uppercut that lifted him off his feet. I knew my fist would ache for a week—if it wasn't broken.

The third footpad, still clutching his groin, stumbled to his feet. My unknown friend whacked him across the backside and sent him scurrying into the dark.

I had my gun out and snapped back the hammer.

"No need for that," said the man with the walking stick. "These ruffians shan't bother anyone else this night."

I said, "You're a handy man to have around. That walking stick of yours packs a good wallop."

He twirled it around and brought it to rest on his shoulder. "It does command a little respect, doesn't it? It's getting so an honest man can't stroll along the waterfront without encountering a ruffian."

He was a heavyset man in a dark frock coat decorated with brass buttons. Muttonchop whiskers framed his round, friendly face. He had on a stovepipe hat.

"The name's Ben Wheeler," I said. "My friend here is Dusty Morgan."

He extended a hand to me and said, "Malachi Petrie at your service, sir."

"You a riverboat captain?" Dusty asked.

Petrie laughed. "A captain? Goodness no, son. A captain is an old lady who sits in his cabin and frets about expenses. On the other hand, son, I am a *pilot*! I *run* the boat! Any river man worth his salt is a pilot! A captain? Never!"

Malachi Petrie dumped three heaping spoons of sugar into his coffee and asked, "Why would any sensible man be looking for Jasper Rollins? The man's a scoundrel!"

He stirred the syrupy liquid.

Suddenly his face lighted up. "Aha! That's it! He *is* a scoundrel and that's why you're looking for him. The man owes you a debt!"

"You could say that," I said, exchanging a look with Dusty. He looked up at me momentarily from his second piece of pie, but he said nothing.

I couldn't tell Petrie that I was looking for Rollins to kill him. I hated betraying his trust. I hated lying to people. I hated this skulking around. I had to find Rollins so that it would be over and done with and I could purge myself of this sickening disease of vengeance that possessed me.

"Well, Mr. Rollins does fancy the *Queen of Natchez*. That's my boat. It's more luxurious than some of the others. Attracts a better crowd. Money, if you know what I mean. Mr. Rollins goes where the money is."

I sipped the hot coffee. I asked casually, "You know where Rollins is now?"

We were sitting in the little cafe down the esplanade from where Dusty and I were attacked. My forehead still ached. It was the second time in a week that I had been beaten up. Dusty's lip puffed up, and he kept a damp cloth to it.

I had discovered a treasure trove better than Jean Laffite's buried swag. This was the first time since we had gotten to St. Louis that I had found a man who admitted he knew Jasper Rollins.

"Last I heard he skedaddled across the river to East St. Louis," Petrie said. "Three, four days ago."

That would be about the time he got word that I was looking for him.

"Things are more wide open in East St. Louis," Petrie explained. "He's probably been in a few games and made himself a stake for the river. That is, if he ain't got himself kilt for cheating."

Petrie looked at me over the top of his coffee cup.

"That man can't cut a deck without cheating. It's in his blood."

I nodded. "So I've heard. Tell me, Mr. Petrie, you planning on taking the *Queen of Natchez* down river any time soon?"

"I certainly am. Ten o'clock sharp tomorrow morning."

"Tomorrow?"

"Ten o'clock sharp." He hesitated. "Well, by noon, anyway. The captain's always procrastinating, waiting for one more passenger, one more load of cargo. He's afraid the general manager's going to ask him why he left port with an empty cabin. So we're always late. Course, he expects me to make up for the lost time on the river."

"You think Rollins'll be aboard when you leave?"

"Like I said, he does fancy the *Queen of Natchez*. Most likely he'll have someone row him over before dawn, and he'll sneak aboard before we leave like the rapscallion he is."

I took a cheroot out of my pocket, bit off the end, and said, "You just let me know if he does. Then I'll see to it that your captain gets two more paying passengers."

I glanced up at the big clock on the side of the packet company office. It said eleven-thirty.

Petrie's captain couldn't procrastinate much longer. Dusty and I stood on the docks waiting to see if we would board the *Queen of Natchez*.

At eleven forty-five Petrie walked to the railing of the texas deck, tipped his stovepipe hat to me, and walked away.

I picked up my satchel, and Dusty and I boarded the stern-wheel riverboat.

Chapter Thirty-One

The next day we passed out of what Malachi Petrie called the Upper River. Below Cairo, its confluence with the Ohio, it became one powerful, meandering river, the Mighty Mississippi!

I was fifteen when I had leisurely floated downriver on Robby O'Bannion's keelboat. In the years since, the river had changed, jumping its banks here, doubling back on itself there. River transportation had changed. Stern-wheelers had replaced the lumbering old side-wheelers. The boats were bigger, faster, safer. The keelboat had vanished forever from the river, driven to oblivion by Robby's detested stinkpots. Even in his own day, Robby was an anachronism. I wondered if he ever learned to accept the riverboats.

"We're in the Lower River," Petrie said in the pilothouse atop the *Queen of Natchez.*

Petrie welcomed Dusty and me into the pilothouse. There were always four or five out-of-work pilots standing around, peering out the big windows. River inspectors, Petrie called them. But there was no question who reigned supreme in this aerie.

"The stretch from St. Looey to Cairo is pretty straight," he said. "Cuts through rocky country. We can run that at night with no problem.

'Tween here and New Orleans the banks are alluvial. River can change overnight."

He pronounced them "Kay-ro" and "Naw Lens."

He wore his black frock coat with every button buttoned. His string tie was neatly tied. I expect he would have worn his tall hat, too, except it would have hit the ceiling.

The pilothouse perched atop the uppermost deck, looking for all the world like an oversized, windowed outhouse. It had a commanding view of the river. From here Petrie was able to read the river and divine meaning from every riffle, ripple, and shadow. He, of course, knew the river by heart, although each trip he had to relearn it because the river was always dynamic, always changing.

"I swear, I ain't never seed the river look the same on any trip," he said. He had both hands on a wheel so big that part of it extended into a slot cut in the deck. Its spokes shined from years of hands gripping the wheel.

"Goin' down, it takes you two hours to get round some elbow. Then comin' up you find the river's cut through the neck of land and there ain't no more elbow. The distance 'tween Cairo and New Orleans is getting shorter. I swear! No lie! In the last two hundred and fifty years the river's shortened itself more'n a mile a year."

Dusty and I spent hours in the pilothouse, absorbing Petrie's tales of such mysteries as chutes and elbows, going inside and going outside, and of quarter twains and mark twains. I laughed at his stories about river inspectors, mud clerks, and alligator boats. He told me how the captain awed people whenever the boat puffed into a river port. He'd have the boiler stokers throw in pitch pine to turn the smoke a fearsome black. I recounted to him the story of my keelboat journey down the river and of my days on the cattle drive and as a marshal.

The novelty quickly wore off for Dusty. There wasn't much romance in the river for him. He frequently curled up in a corner of the pilothouse with his dime novels. Oftentimes he simply fell asleep.

I felt a pang when I thought of how much Abby would have enjoyed riding a riverboat. The view from the wheelhouse of the flat prairies, the rolling plains, the high bluffs, and the wooded areas along the riverbank was spectacular. The river itself was a living thing: beautiful, mysterious, beckoning, dangerous. Abby had known little luxury in life. The *Queen of Natchez* was like an elegant, floating hotel, with waiters to serve delicious meals and maids to turn down your bed covers at night.

But she could not be beside me. And the last instrument of her removal was within my grasp.

I didn't spot Rollins until the second night.

Petrie said he would sometimes hole up in his cabin with plantation owners and cotton brokers and not emerge until he had cleaned them out or the trip was over.

I hoped that would not be the case here. I planned to do more than simply shoot Rollins. I wanted to expose him as a cheat, and I wanted it to be as public as possible.

He was playing poker at a table in the large, noisy, smoky main salon. He wore a black cutaway coat, and a beaver hat was on his head. He had on a lacy pink shirt, string tie, and a brocaded vest. The ruffled shirt-sleeves extended out beyond his coat sleeves. His red beard and mustache and his round, cheerful face gave him a benign appearance. He looked for all the world like a rube in his Sunday-go-to-meetin' best. It was a disarming illusion that I felt certain he cultivated to lull his prey into overconfidence.

I watched him from a distance. Every now and then he spread his knees, as though stretching or searching for a more comfortable position. Each time he did, it activated the holdout and placed a card deftly in his palm. The ruffled sleeve helped hide it. He was quite slick about it.

None of his opponents had spotted it. I detected it because I knew what to look for. Doc Holliday had described to me how it worked.

Petrie joined me, and I said, "That's an ingenious device he's got there. It's known as a Kepplinger holdout. When he wants a card, he spreads his knees and that yanks on a cord. Runs up to his shoulders through tubes and pulleys, and darned if a card doesn't pop into his hand."

"I always knew he was crooked," Petrie said. "Never could prove it. Least till now. I'll tell the captain and have him put ashore immediately. The captain don't allow no cheaters on board. Neither do I."

"Hold your horses," I said. "I'll take care of the man."

Petrie looked at me. "You sure?"

"Why do you think I've been looking for him?"

Petrie kept looking at me. "I reckon maybe you can at that."

Maybe I could, but I knew he would not be an easy man to take. He was a man who practiced deceit and deception. I wondered if he would recognize it when it was practiced on him.

Petrie, I noticed, was a cautious and meticulous man in the wheelhouse. He had an awesome responsibility. It was his keen eyes and prodigious memory that saw the *Queen of Natchez* safely through the shoal waters and past the snags that clotted the constantly shifting riverbed.

But away from the wheelhouse he was open and gregarious. We drank whiskey and smoked cigars and watched the people around us. Dusty had long since crawled into the upper bunk in the tiny cabin we shared.

I felt the deck vibrating under my feet, an ever-present reminder of the clanking connecting rods turning the stern wheel. If you stepped outside, away from the din of the gamblers, you could hear the chuff-chuff of the boilers and the ringing of the watch bell in the pilothouse.

"Who's at the wheel?" I asked. "One of them deadheading river inspectors?"

Petrie looked at me and smiled maliciously around the cigar in his mouth. Then he removed it and said, "I wouldn't let one of them hold my coat. My cub's at the wheel. He fancies himself a lightning pilot. The likes of Mr. Horace Bixby he'll never be, but he's a fair lad at the wheel. Learnin' fast."

"Good teacher," I said, laughing.

Petrie raised his whiskey glass to me. "Well, I sure ain't gonna argue with that."

Petrie drifted off to bed for a few hours of sleep before his next watch.

I watched Rollins. He didn't win every hand. That would have been suspicious. But he won enough to make him a consistent winner. The pile of chips in front of him grew ever larger during the night.

Rollins sat across the plush green table from me and said, "Gentlemen, a friendly game of bluff. Poker to you. Five-card stud. My deal."

I had a cup of after-breakfast coffee and a pile of chips in front of me. Dusty stood behind me. There were nine players seated at the table.

"What'll it be, gentlemen?" Rollins asked. "What's the limit? A penny?"

"A penny?" said one man with a guffaw. "Maybe we should play for matchsticks."

Another said, "I thought we were playing a man's game."

Rollins shrugged. "Ten cents?" he offered.

"Gentlemen," a fourth man said, "let's at least make it interestin'. This is a game of skill we playin'. I think a couple of rounds and we'll eliminate any greenhorns. How 'bout twenty-five cents?"

Rollins quickly agreed to the increased limit.

The fourth man said, "Maybe later we can raise it to make it even more interestin'."

My bet was this was a man who bore watching as closely as Rollins. I suspected they were in it together.

Rollins held a deck in his left hand. Three fingers were on the edge of the long side, and the index finger was at the outer right corner. It's called a mechanic's grip. He quickly and expertly dealt cards to the nine players at the table.

First he dealt the cards that go facedown on the table. The hole cards. The mechanic's grip allows the dealer to take a peak at the cards as he flips them out or to deal from the bottom of the deck.

He was too fast and too good for anyone to detect any shenanigans. Once again I had been warned by Doc Holliday what to look for.

Rollins dealt the first round of face-up cards and called for bets.

My face-up card was a five of hearts. I looked at my hole card: the nine of clubs.

Rollins's face-up card was the king of hearts. Two other players had kings. One had a queen.

I didn't bid anything. On the next round I got a ten of diamonds. I folded.

A cotton planter from Louisiana won the pot with two pair. I could see it was going to be a long day.

By the fifth game I was down fifteen dollars and had not won a pot. Or come close. The man I suspected of being Rollins's partner won two hands. A cotton broker won one and Rollins took one.

Dusty drifted away after that. I don't blame him.

We played until nearly three o'clock in the afternoon. I was fifty dollars in the hole. The only consistent winner was Rollins's "partner," a man we had come to know as Mr. Fowler. He said he was in the factoring business in New Orleans.

Rollins raked in the cards and said, "Shall we meet here after supper? Say seven o'clock?"

"Sounds good to me," said Fowler. "But I suggest we sweeten the pot. Make it a little more interestin'."

"I dunno," said one of the players. "It's already kinda rich for my blood."

Fowler laughed. "I said we'd eventually scare out the greenhorns."

Chapter Thirty-Two

Immediately after supper we gathered in the main salon to play cards. Three of our players didn't show up, but a new man joined us.

As we sat down, a waiter delivered a tray with two bottles of Kentucky sour mash bourbon, glasses, and two new decks of cards.

"I took the liberty of orderin', gentlemen," said Rollins. "Help yourself. If you'd rather brandy, I've got a tab at the bar."

Fowler rubbed his hands together. "Gents, tonight we're gonna play a *real* man's game!"

"High-stakes poker?" said Rollins. "That sounds mighty interestin'!"

Rollins looked at me and shoved over a new deck of cards. "Would you do us the honor of cuttin' the deck, Mr.—er, Morgan, ain't it?"

"That's right," I said. "Morgan. Algernon Morgan."

I was glad Dusty wasn't there. That was his real name, and if he heard anybody using it he would have died of embarrassment. I passed myself off as a cattleman who had just sold his herd in Kansas. It wasn't too big a lie.

I cut the deck and handed it back to Rollins.

"I hope you feelin' lucky tonight, Mr. Morgan," he said. "Gentlemen, pour y'self a drink and let's begin."

* * *

I studied my hand, then reached down to finger the rabbit's foot Dusty had given me.

I tossed out two blue chips. "I'll see your two hundred, Mr. Rollins."

I threw two more chips into the pile. "And I'll raise you two hundred."

I looked at my hand again. I had three of a kind. It was the best hand I'd had all night. My face-up cards were the nine of diamonds and the nine of spades, six of clubs and the jack of spades. My hole card was the nine of hearts.

I'd been losing steadily all night. Fowler had won several hands. But this time Rollins was the big winner.

"Well, gentlemen," Rollins said.

The cotton broker on my right flipped his cards over facedown. "I fold," he said.

The tobacco merchant next to him folded, too. So did the others, until it was just Rollins, a cotton planter, and me.

The cotton planter peeked at his hole card again. He said, "You got a mighty pleased look on your face, Mr. Rollins. Let's see if you got something to back it up."

The planter, whose name was Tatum, had the makings of a straight. Showing, he had a five of hearts, a four of clubs, a three of diamonds, and a two of clubs. If his hole card was an ace, he might have it.

But Rollins had the makings of a flush. He had the king, jack, ten, and nine of clubs on the table. If his hole card was a queen of clubs, he had the pot again.

But it was a big if, and he could be bluffing.

Rollins took a long swig of whiskey, then said, "Mr. Tatum, I'll be happy to oblige. But it's going to cost you the pot."

Tatum turned over his hole card. It *was* an ace. He had me beat.

Tatum had a big smile on his face as he reached for the pot.

Rollins watched him, then said, "Pardon me, Mr. Tatum, but I do believe you're being hasty. You haven't seen my hole card yet."

The chances that Rollins had a queen were astronomical—that is, if he was playing fair. I had watched him closely. I saw him work the holdout several times and come up with the right card. I had no doubt now that his hole card was a queen.

Rollins turned over the card. It was a queen.

"King-high straight flush," he said, smiling triumphantly.

Tatum's face reddened as he stared at Rollins. "You seem to have a lot of luck, Mr. Rollins. That's the third straight pot you've won with mighty fancy cards."

The smile vanished from Rollins's face.

He said evenly, "Mr. Tatum, luck has nothin' to do with it. If you don't realize that poker is a game of skill and not of chance, then, sir, I think you are playing the wrong game!"

The flush on Tatum's face deepened. His mouth tightened. I waited to see if he would make a play.

He didn't, so I knew it was up to me.

I said, "Gentlemen, I think Mr. Rollins is right. Poker is a game of skill."

Fowler agreed. "It ain't no place for greenhorns, thas fer sure."

Rollins beamed across the table at me. His hands reached for the pile of chips.

"Mr. Rollins is quite skilled in the art of poker," I continued blandly. His smile widened.

"And in the art of cheating."

His smile quickly turned to a frown. Then a black scowl. He slowly moved his hands away from the pot, back toward the edge of the table.

I guessed that Rollins had a bellybuster derringer hidden somewhere in his ruffled shirt. He would go for it soon enough. But his hands were still on the table.

"I'll kill you for that!" he snarled.

I stood up and flipped my coattail away from my holstered gun. He eyed the .45 resting in the holster and figured the odds. Rollins was a gambler, but he never took chances.

Out of the corner of my eye I saw Fowler start to work his way behind me. He pretended to be trying to get a better look.

I said, "Mr. Fowler, would please stay where I can see you."

He moved back.

If Rollins went for his gun, I could shoot him dead and it would be over. I'd probably have to shoot Fowler, too.

I didn't think Rollins would, and he didn't. He decided, instead, to play out his bluff.

His hands were back on the pile of chips. He said, "I believe this is mine. You gentlemen saw me. Did I cheat? Feel the cards. Do you feel any pinpricks? Examine them. Do you see any marks? Have they been shaved or cut in any way?"

Several of the players examined the cards. "No marks that I can see," said one.

Rollins nodded his head. "I've encountered sore losers before," he said. "But I do believe this . . . this gentleman is the limit."

Now was the time for me to play out my bluff.

I said, "Ask Mr. Rollins to spread his legs."

The other players looked at me strangely. Tatum said, "I beg your pardon, sir?"

I moved behind Rollins and motioned for Fowler to stay in my line of sight. I said to Rollins, "Keep your hands on the table and spread your legs!"

He looked up at me. His eyes were a blank. The man was a poker player to the end.

If my bluff failed, if Rollins wasn't wearing the Kepplinger holdout, I'd just as well swim to shore.

I repeated my command, but Rollins didn't move.

I said, "Either you spread your legs, Mr. Rollins, or I will do it for you! And may I remind you to keep your hands on the table! And Mr. Fowler, I want you to keep your hands where I can see them!"

Rollins began to open his legs.

"Wider!" I ordered.

He opened his legs wide. His hands were on the table, palms down.

Tatum said, "I don't see no card!"

The cotton planter looked at me and scolded, "This has been a regrettable demonstration, sir! No gentleman would behave in such a fashion!"

I had to play it out. I said, "Ask him to turn over his hand."

Rollins turned his right hand palm up. It was empty.

"The other hand!"

The hand turned over slowly. It was curled into a tight fist.

"If you please, sir," said Tatum.

The fingers slowly uncurled.

In his fist was a crumpled card.

The next morning I returned Dusty's rabbit foot. It had brought me good luck. I thanked Dusty and said I hoped it would continue to bring him good luck.

"I tol' you it'd work, din' I, Ben?" he said proudly.

"You were right, Dusty. It worked."

He kissed the furry rabbit's foot and put it into a pocket.

Petrie, his eyes on the ripples revealing the presence of a shoal reef a hundred yards downriver, said, "Mr. Rollins will never play on the river again. The man's a pariah now. No one will play with him. I doubt if any steamboat company'll book his passage."

I said, "That's the risk you take in poker."

Turning the boat expertly away from the shoal, Petrie said, "I always suspected he was up to no good. But I never knew for sure."

There was a straight course of river ahead. Petrie beckoned Dusty to the wheel.

"Put both hands on 'er and hold 'er steady as she goes," he said.

Dusty grasped the wheel. "Like this, Mr. Petrie?"

"By golly, I think you got it," he said. "I'll make a lightnin' pilot of you yet."

"A lightnin' pilot! Did y'hear that, Ben?"

I laughed. "I heard, Dusty. A lightning pilot."

I had lost all desire to kill Jasper Rollins. I had had enough of vengeance. It takes its toll on the avenger, as well as the victim.

I thought Rollins would slink off the boat at the next stop and probably make his way to Natchez-Under-the-Hill.

After I had seen the scorn heaped upon him in the salon last night, my determination to kill him had vanished. He had been exposed as a scoundrel. He could no longer work the riverboats. His reputation would follow him wherever he went. He couldn't return to Dodge City. Wyatt Earp was a gambler himself, and neither he nor Doc Holliday had any tolerance for cheaters.

I doubted that he could return to robbing banks. He had no talent for that at all.

I had no desire to kill him. His ruined reputation and livelihood were greater punishment.

No doubt he would disappear to lick his wounds.

The one thing I didn't count on was that Rollins's sense of self-preservation vanished with his reputation.

That night, the last night before we were due to arrive in New Orleans, he and Fowler tried to bushwhack me in the dark on the texas deck.

They might have succeeded if anxiety hadn't gotten the better of them.

Fowler fired too soon and too carelessly. He should have waited a few more seconds.

The shot missed. It tore into a doorjamb and threw off a shower of splinters.

I didn't miss. Fowler dropped to the deck like a sack of grain unloaded by a roustabout.

"Don't shoot! Don't shoot!" Rollins cried in anguish.

He staggered out into the open, his hands raised high. He stepped over the body of his fallen henchman. "I give up!" he blubbered. "Don't shoot!"

I said, "How did Bill Smoot ever tie up with a sniveling coward like you?"

The color drained from his face. "You th' one!" he said in near panic. "You the one what kilt th' Kid and Bill! You th' one what been askin' 'bout me in St. Looey! How come? What y'got agin us?"

"Remember San Miguel, Jasper?" I said harshly. "Remember the woman you killed in the bank. That woman was my wife!"

"I din' kill 'er!" he blubbered. "It was Kid Bayliss! He done it! I was outside wit' the' horses! Doan kill me! Oh, God, doan kill me!"

I holstered my gun and said, "You ain't worth the price of a bullet!"

Dusty came racing down the stairs. "I heard the shots. You all right, Ben?"

He ran right into Rollins, and the tinhorn grabbed him around the neck with his left arm.

Rollins kicked out one leg and a derringer popped into his right hand. He pressed it against the back of Dusty's head. Rollins was always a man for a holdout.

"One move," Rollins snarled, "an' yore frien' is a dead man!"

The gun was a Remington .41-caliber derringer, known as an "over-and-under" because of its two barrels, one on top of the other. It was a small gun, but it packed a wallop. Each bullet weighed a hundred and thirty grains.

"Doan worry 'bout me," Dusty said bravely.

"You hurt Dusty and I'll—"

"You ain't gonna do nothin'!" he cried, the panic still in his voice. "Take out your gun real easy like and put it on the deck."

I lifted it out with my thumb and forefinger. I bent over and set it on the deck.

"Now kick it over to me," he instructed.

Before I could respond, Dusty twisted away from Rollins.

The three-inch barrel belched fire and smoke. The report was sharp and loud.

Dusty clutched at his chest and fell to the deck. He made a kind of "Ooof!" sound.

"You son of a bitch!" I screamed as I scooped up my gun.

Rollins swung the little belly gun toward me.

I fired twice and hit him twice. I fired again for Dusty. The bastard had shot Dusty!

Rollins fell backward, sprawling half over his henchman's body. One leg kicked up, then he was still.

I bent over Dusty. "Dusty! Dusty!" I cried.

I cradled him in my arms. I was about to bawl like a baby.

Dusty stirred in my arms.

"Wha—?" He clutched at his chest. "My chest," he said faintly. "It hurts like hell!"

I pulled open his shirt. He had a folded wad of dime novels tucked into his front.

I picked up the wad. Rollins's bullet was embedded in the books. It had not gone through.

"It hurts somethin' powerful," Dusty said.

"I 'spect you're gonna have a good bruise," I said. "You are one lucky man!"

He cocked one eye at me and said, "It was th' rabbit's foot! I know it was!"

I wasn't going to argue.

It was over. Montana Smith, Kid Bayliss, Bill Smoot, Jasper Rollins. All dead.

I felt no sense of satisfaction. I felt no sense of justice. What I had done would not bring Abby back. It was just something I had to do. Now I could get on with my life.

Dusty and I rode west from New Orleans.

I wondered if I would accept that offer from Angus.

Or had the passion for vengeance and the gun set me upon a course from which I could not turn back?

The answer lay on the trail ahead.